P9-EML-981

The Dragons of Spratt, Ohio

WITHDRAWN
LVC BISHOP LIBRARY

The Dragons
of Spratt, Ohio

Linda Zinnen

HarperCollins*Publishers*

The Dragons of Spratt, Ohio
Copyright © 2004 by Linda Zinnen
All rights reserved. No part of this book may be used or reproduced
in any manner whatsoever without written permission except in the case of
brief quotations embodied in critical articles and reviews.
Printed in the United States of America. For information address
HarperCollins Children's Books, a division of HarperCollins Publishers,
1350 Avenue of the Americas, New York, NY 10019.
www.harperchildrens.com

Library of Congress Cataloging-in-Publication Data
Zinnen, Linda.
The dragons of Spratt, Ohio / by Linda Zinnen.—1st ed.
    p.   cm.
Summary: Seventh-grader John Salt, a budding animal behaviorist, and his
best friend's sister become unlikely allies in an attempt to protect a pack of
dragons from an unscrupulous cosmetics researcher.
    ISBN 0-06-000021-X — ISBN 0-06-000022-8 (lib. bdg.)
    [1. Dragons—Fiction.   2. Animal refuges—Fiction.   3. Cosmetics
industry—Fiction.   4. Aunts—Fiction.   5. Ohio—Fiction.]   I Title.
PZ76545 Dr   2004   2003019610
[Fic]—dc22

Typography by Nicole de las Heras
1   2   3   4   5   6   7   8   9   10
❖
First Edition

For Sarah, Rachel, and Hannah,
my fabulous daughters

The Dragons of Spratt, Ohio

Chapter One

—m—

"**Y**ep. There she goes," John Salt said to his dad. He rolled down the Jeep's window on the passenger side and stuck his head and shoulders into the misty air of a wet afternoon in late February.

"Here," his dad said, handing him a set of binoculars. "Is she circling?"

Salt—nobody but his family called him John anymore—rested his elbow on the door and trained the binoculars on the slow-moving blot in the gray sky. "Uh-huh. She's flying pretty low over the wheyr. I keep losing her behind the hills."

He put his left hand over the binoculars, shading the lenses to keep off the drizzle. "She must be about twenty feet off the ground. Her wings are really pulling hard. She's not getting much help from the wind today. Any lower and her tail spikes are gonna drag on the ground."

"Hmm," his dad said thoughtfully. "Dr. Zhao wrote something about the circling behavior of the postovipositional female."

Salt's dad pulled out a thick airmail envelope and paged through the Chinese dragonologist's letter. His dad liked to read aloud from Dr. Zhao's letter every chance he got. And Salt liked to listen. Frankly, Dr. Zhao was a genius.

"Yeah, here it is. 'Once the breeding female has delivered her eggs, she will rise to circle the nest, beating at the air—'"

"You should see the treetops bending," said Salt. "She's really kicking up a breeze."

"'—which dissipates the dragonstink and thus serves to hide the nest from egg-sucking predators. Does Ohio have egg-sucking predators?'"

"Raccoons," said Salt. Though he had answered the question a hundred times before, he felt like answering it again. Hey, it wasn't every day a guy's personal hero wondered, "Does Ohio have egg-sucking predators?" A question that big and important deserved an answer every time. "Opossums, snakes. Nothing big enough to tackle one of these eggs, *that's* for sure."

His dad grinned his agreement and kept reading. "'After several passes, the dragon will overfly her entire territory one last time before nightfall, after which she will return to the wheyr to complete her life cycle. *Do* be terribly careful not to disturb the incubating eggs in the coming days, won't you?'"

"Oh, we will," Salt assured Dr. Zhao's letter. "We'll be careful. Real, real—hang on, Dad. She's found an updraft."

He watched the Chinese flying dragon stretch to her maximum wingspan. Even the gray light of a drizzly winter sky couldn't dim the translucent shine of her greenish gold wing membranes, or hide the powerful arch of her neck and spine. The dragon caught the wind and began to soar. Salt shivered.

"She's rising, John," said Salt's dad hoarsely. "And she's laid her eggs. According to Dr. Zhao, she doesn't have long now." He sniffed, and wiped his eyes with a corner of Dr. Zhao's letter.

Salt swallowed hard. "Good-bye," he whispered as the matriarch rose into the sky. She circled the wheyr again, then sailed out of sight among the misty clouds.

Salt ducked back into the Jeep. "She was my first dragon," he said wistfully, still staring out his open window. "I'll never forget her."

"Yeah," said his dad. "Boy. It's gonna be anticlimactic, going back to doctoring plain old warthogs and yaks until her eggs hatch, huh? But then we'll have our very own dragon pack right here at the Wilds." And he rubbed his hands together gleefully.

Salt grinned at his dad, the large-animal vet for the International Center for the Preservation of Wildlife—the Wilds. Twenty years ago Central Ohio Coal donated fourteen square miles of reclaimed strip mines just south of Spratt, Ohio, for use as a wild animal refuge. Since then the Wilds had evolved into the San Diego Zoo of the Midwest, the Serengeti of southeastern Ohio. All sorts of exotic animals roamed the Wilds' ponds and pastures—egrets and emus, rhinos and gazelles, giraffes and oryxes. And what was left of the poor zebra herd, of course.

During the summer months, the Wilds really jumped. Thousands of tourists rode safari busses through the pastures, snapping pictures of free-ranging musk oxen. Zookeepers and field researchers from all over the world packed the Wilds' zoological conferences on the latest breakthroughs in endangered-animal management. And last year's Eco-Run broke all marathon attendance records.

Winter was pretty quiet, though. The tourists headed for Florida, the field researchers went back to the field, and the Wilds lay silent under a thin blanket of snow. Most of the animals spent their days inside the heated animal barns. Even on mild, sunny days, only the zebras ventured out into the south corral next to the deserted picnic shelters. They stood around and shivered, wondering when the heck it was going to warm up.

Salt figured the zebras were the reason the dragon had decided to stay. The matriarch came gliding over Spratt one clear morning in January, so high and silent, she barely cast a shadow on the rooftops. Eight thousand miles from home, but she certainly liked what she saw down below—all those tasty zebras bunched together in the corral. Dinner in a box.

The dragon had burrowed into this remote hill next to the barbed-wire fence that separated the grassy Wilds from the unreclaimed coal lands to the west. She promptly began eating her way through the zebra herd. The director of the Wilds had gone ballistic as one expensive zebra after another disappeared down the dragon's gullet.

As Salt pulled out his observation notebook and a pencil, a pair of headlights glinted in the Jeep's rearview mirror. He turned and squinted through the fogged-up back window. A rusty orange pickup had topped the hill and was driving down the dirt track into the pasture. A pickup that orange (and that rusty) belonged to only one person. The director of the Wilds had arrived.

"Mom's here," said Salt.

The pickup bumped to a stop next to the Jeep. Salt's mom rolled down her window. "I'm late! I'm late!" she called. "Did I miss anything?"

"She's laid her eggs and flown off to . . ." Salt's voice trailed off. He swallowed hard.

His mom shook her head sadly. "Shoot. I wanted to say *'Vaya con Dios'* before she . . . I swear, those appropriations meetings just go on and on."

"Sorry, Mom."

"Yeah." She opened her door and stepped out into the drizzle. "Well. We can't do a thing for the mama, right? Soooo . . . let's check out the eggs!"

Salt's dad grabbed a flashlight from the backseat of the Jeep and got out. "Did you bring a raincoat, SueAnn?"

"Uh-huh. Boots, too." Salt's mom flipped open the carryall bolted to the truck bed. She took off her high heels and backhanded them through the truck's opened window. "John?" she said, zipping a raincoat over her bright red business suit. "You coming?"

Salt got out of the Jeep, scribbling in his notebook. "Did we get out here at four twenty or four thirty, Dad?"

"Four twenty, I think."

"Got it." Salt jotted down the time. Then he drew a small sketch in the margin: the matriarch soaring into the misty clouds. A graceful one-line drawing of parting and sweet sorrow—until his mom bumped his elbow. The dragon's tail skittered off the page.

"Do you realize we are going to be the first western-ers to *see* dragon eggs? I'm so excited I'm gonna bust!" She smooched Salt's dad hard on the lips and strode off into the gathering darkness. "C'mon, guys. This way."

It was hard to keep up with his tall, long-legged par-ents. Salt was neither tall nor long legged. He took after the Dinsmore side of the family: kind of short, kind of freckly, kind of slow. Built more for comfort than for speed. Salt broke into a lumbering trot.

"So," said Salt's dad, "what did the Appropriations Committee say about my requisition for more zebras?"

Salt's mom snorted. "That darned dragon ate twelve zebras. Twelve! Replacing all twelve zebras at once is impossible, Peter. That would put the South African pas-tures way over the quarterly budget."

"But the zebras are a big draw," protested Salt's dad. "We can't go into the tourist season with a skimpy little herd. Besides, the damage could have been a lot worse. At least our zebras aren't endangered. Dr. Zhao said that dragons have been known to go after pandas."

"Your Holstein theory worked out great, Dad," puffed Salt. "Substituting cows for zebras. Sheer genius."

His dad smiled modestly. "It's the perfect food chain for southeast Ohio. Thistle to Holstein to dragon. And cows are cheap at county auction. The Wilds has miles of grasslands to feed 'em. Once the eggs hatch, we'll raise the dragonlings on cow right from the start.

"Soooo, I've been thinking, SueAnn. I bet we could buy . . . nine zebras out of the Wilds' rainy day fund."

"Nine zebras?" spluttered his mom. "Get outa here! Two's more like it."

"Eight."

"Two and a half."

"C'mon, SueAnn, play fair! What am I supposed to do with half a zebra?"

His parents dickered the entire way. Salt was so used to hearing his parents yak on about the Wilds' budget that he tuned them out and thought about supper instead. He was starving. Sure, he wanted to see the dragon eggs, but he couldn't wait to get home and dry off. Warm up. Eat three helpings and stretch out on the familiar comfort of the couch and flip on the TV. There was never anything good on Tuesday nights, but that was okay, because he could always watch a nature documentary or two from his video collection. His favorite? *Dragons: From Myth to Reality*, filmed at the research station in China and narrated by Salt's personal hero, the great Dr. Zhao himself.

The video was so cool. The dragons were amazing, of course. And Dr. Zhao was not just a zoological genius but everything a field researcher ought to be: humble, modest, and brave. Boy. The way Dr. Zhao explained dragonic digestion; the way he inspected an abandoned wheyr; the way he jumped clear of a tail swipe aimed in his direction. Salt shook his head in awe. It takes a lot of courage to annoy a dragon. You really had to admire the guy—at least, Salt had to. Maybe he'd rewind and watch *Dragons* twice tonight.

And maybe, just maybe, if he watched his hero explain, inspect, and jump out of the way twice tonight, Salt would finally work up the courage to modestly, humbly, *bravely* pick up the phone, call Allison Fishbinder—only the most incredibly beautiful girl in Spratt—and ask her to the seventh grade dance.

Hope squeezed his heart. He could almost hear Allison coo, "Sure, Salt. Of *course* I'd love to go to the dance with you."

Salt grinned happily, completely forgetting that his imagination (like his freckles) hailed from the Dinsmore side of the family. It was a wonderful imagination— wide-ranging and optimistic, a real life-enriching personal characteristic. It just had a couple of little blind spots. Like the fact that Allison Fishbinder would sooner eat a worm than go to the dance with John Salt.

Salt sighed with satisfaction, so busy twirling the beauteous Allison across the gym floor that he barely noticed the weird bounce beneath his boots. Reclaimed strip mine was like that. Like walking on spongy concrete. Though some of the animal technicians worried about sinkholes and groundwater erosion and subsidence out here, Salt never did. He conserved his mental energy for important stuff, like his first dance with Allison (a waltz? a tango? the Macarena, perhaps?), and what they were having for supper tonight, and how tired his feet were, and—

"Four," announced his mom as they climbed the slope toward the entrance to the wheyr. "Take it or leave it."

Salt's dad sighed. "You drive a hard bargain, SueAnn."

"That's why I am the big chief pencil pusher, sweetie." She dropped back, linked arms with Salt, and winked. "I woulda paid for six," she gloated. "I just saved a bundle."

They stopped at the entrance of the wheyr—a perfectly circular, perfectly deep, perfectly dark hole four feet in diameter halfway up the hill, not far from the barbed-wire fence that separated the Wilds from unreclaimed land. Salt's dad clicked on his flashlight and pointed the beam down the slanted wyrmhole.

"I can't see a thing," said Salt. "No. Wait." A glint of gold made him kneel eagerly at the edge of the wyrmhole. His mom crouched behind him, her hand warm on his neck, as his dad trained the light over their heads.

"Wow," breathed Salt. "Just—*wow*." Nine golden eggs glistened in the nest of old cow bones and branches daubed with mud in the middle of the earthen chamber.

"Yeah," said his dad softly, "wow. There's nothing more mysteriously profound than an incubating egg. Gives me goose bumps every time."

"We are gonna treat you sweet babies like royalty," crooned Salt's mom. "We are gonna appropriate the finest Holsteins, the best climbing trees, the sunniest glades—"

"Five whole zebras for your favorite vet," crooned Salt's dad.

"Ha! Don't push me, pal." She stood and wiped her muddy hands on the grass. "Gosh. It's so peaceful out here." She sighed. "No phones, no faxes, no fund-raising. I ought to get out in the field more often."

Salt stood up too. "You work too hard, Mom," he said. "Seriously. Why don't you blow off the paperwork tonight and hang out in front of the TV with me? We could . . ." Salt took a deep breath. His dreams dimmed a little, dreams of watching his personal hero and work-ing up the guts to call Allison, but hey, this was for his mom. "We could watch *Titanic*."

Salt's mom tilted her face to the drizzly sky and threw her arms wide. "Hold me, Jack! I'm flying!" She dropped her hands and grinned at Salt. "What a great idea, sweetie. You're the best."

Salt took one last, lingering look at the wyrmhole. He wouldn't have missed this moment for anything. The thrill! The excitement! The challenge of what lay ahead!

He checked his watch. And if they hurried home, he'd have time to make a big bowl of cheddar and bacon popcorn before the big boat sailed away.

Chapter Two

—⚭—

"**Y**ou're gonna poke your eye out with that thing, Birdbrain," observed Ham Clarke.

"Shut up," replied Candi.

Candi Clarke finished her left eyelid, blinked twice at the reassuringly pretty reflection in the pocket mirror, then licked the pointy tip of her eyeliner pencil and started on her other eyelid. "You're gonna make me mess up. Then I'd have to start all over, and the bus is gonna be here in five minutes."

Boy, oh boy, oh boy. Of all the twin brothers in the world, she had to get stuck with Ham. Ham was twelve minutes younger and twelve minutes dumber. That was all there was to it.

The notebook clamped between Candi's knees started to slip. She juggled her makeup supplies as she bent over and hiked it more firmly between her legs.

Mornings would be a whole lot easier if her mom would just let her wear more than a dab of blush and lip gloss to school. If only she could apply eyeliner in the comfort of the bathroom and not out here at the chilly, windy bus stop. Didn't her mom realize that according to *Makeup from the Edge*, the international style magazine of makeup, classically outlined eyes were back in style? Didn't her mom *care*?

Well, no, she didn't. So Candi was totally stuck. Doomed to do a sloppy, last-minute eyeliner job at the bus stop every morning. And the hairstyle she had planned would never survive in this wind. Life was so unfair.

"Hey, Salt," said Ham as John Salt, Ham's best friend and the only other kid at Spratt Grammar who lived out this far, walked up.

"Hey, Ham, hey, Candi," Salt said excitedly. "We checked out the wheyr last night and we've got nine eggs!"

"Nine dragon eggs. Whoa," said Ham.

Grimly, Candi pushed and pulled at her frizzy brown hair, coaxing it into a topknot. She jammed in a couple of her favorite rhinestone hair clips, sparkly pink dragonflies, and checked the mirror. Hey, she looked good. Great, even. Just great.

She sighed as she stowed her makeup supplies in her

purse. She had never looked better—or felt more bummed. What? What? *What* had she done to deserve the terrible direction her life had taken? Zip, zero, nothing. All she had done was sit down to take the first math test of seventh grade back in September. She had been calm, she had been collected, she had been ready to perform at her usual C-plus level—but instead of slowly scratching her way through the steps for the first question:

$$solve\ for\ x:\ 2(x - 17) + 3x = 126$$

her brain had simply whispered, "Thirty-two."

And ba-boom! All the random bits of information—math facts and landforms and the Treaty of Versailles and comma splices—everything anyone had ever tried to teach her fell like pinballs into the correct slots. Her brain lit up like a scoreboard during the bonus round. All those years of school and finally she knew what the teachers were talking about! Everything made sense!

Candi got a big fat A on that test—the first A she'd ever gotten in math. But it wasn't just math. English was a breeze. Science was easy as spit. She slung her purse over her shoulder and glanced at Salt.

"Yeah, I'm kinda nervous, though," said Salt to Ham. "What if there's a dud egg? Happens all the time, Dr. Zhao says."

Candi rolled her eyes. Sure, being smart was fun at first. She never had to study (not that she ever did before), and she did great. Her first report card that year was amazing. Her parents were soooo happy. Her mom had baked her this really amazing cake in the shape of the Parthenon, and her dad had started leaving Ohio State University brochures under her cereal bowl every morning. Of course, she rubbed Ham's nose in her straight-A report cards every nine weeks. Was there even a downside to being smart?

Unfortunately—yes.

Candi started to read—and not just makeup magazines, either. Reading was like discovering the power of the perfect shade of lip gloss; only instead of enhancing and defining her slightly thin lips, she was filling in the contours of her mind. Aristotle's *Poetics*. *Lives of a Cell*. *Everything That Rises Must Converge*. *Twenty Thousand Leagues Under the Sea* and on one long, rainy Sunday afternoon when she had a headache anyway, Candi lay across her bed and read her evolutionary biology textbook cover to cover, footnotes included, while listening to a Brahms concerto on her headphones.

But it wasn't until she picked up a slim blue volume called *Discours de la méthode pour bien conduire sa raison et chercher la vérité dans les sciences*, by a guy named René

Descartes (ooo, cute name, huh?), that things really got out of hand.

"*'Cogito, ergo sum,'*" she murmured. "I think, therefore I am. That's it exactly! How did this Descartes guy ever know? Wow. Just—*wow.*"

Amazing book. Because of it, Candi fell head over heels in love with everything French—philosophy, history, music, architecture. It didn't hurt that the French always looked fabulous, so natural in beautiful clothes and perfect hairstyles whatever the social occasion. Take the seventeenth century, for instance. Who else would have the guts to build a Hall of Mirrors except the French, who sailed through life knowing they looked terrific from any angle? Candi really admired that.

Reading up about the clothes, the hair, the Hall of Mirrors—that part was fine. But what wasn't fine was how she'd been spending time actually thinking about the stuff she read. Thinking—what kind of geeky thing was *that* to do? It wasn't so bad when she managed to keep her thoughts to herself. But lately every single topic at school was totally fascinating. Polynomials. Protozoans. The pyramids at Giza. She found herself raising her hand and making insightful little comments in English class, in science class, in the lunch line, everywhere. Her teachers were nodding and smiling, so happy to have somebody actually pay attention. Her friends, on the other hand, were staring in utter disbelief. They were beginning to talk. She had to get a grip.

Candi glanced at Salt as she gave her bangs a final fluff, irritated all over again. Jeez. Just listen to him, standing there yakking away about those stupid dragons. Didn't Salt realize how weird it made him, to be interested in something other than sports and horsing around at school? Didn't he care that while all the popular kids were out playing baseball and getting detentions, he had his nose stuck in his notebook drawing dragon snouts?

Candi sighed. Her friends thought Salt was a weenie to be so totally wrapped up with the dragons. Dragons were for little kids. Here they were, teenagers, practically. It was time to put away childish things—things like dragons, and getting all wrapped up in reading and thinking, and neglecting, sometimes, your role as a pretty and popular person.

Good grief. If she didn't get a grip soon, if she didn't get *unwrapped* from all the deeply interesting reading and thinking she'd been doing on the sly lately, she, Candi Clarke, currently the second-most-popular girl in Spratt, was headed for seventh-grade weeniedom. And no one who had ever experienced the joy and happiness that came from running around with the people who matter would ever voluntarily fall off Planet Popular.

Eat lunch with the weird kids. Be picked last in gym. Become clueless when talking to members of the opposite sex. Wear icky clothes.

Just like Salt.

Candi crossed her arms and glared at Salt. "Okay, I'm gonna ask," she said. "What is that all over the front of your shirt?"

"What, this?" asked Salt, pulling at the front of his *Animals Are People Too* T-shirt and frowning at the dark splotches. "Dirt. I think."

"Uh-huh. And *please* don't tell me that's what I think it is all over your boots." Candi rolled her eyes and pointed one apricot-polished fingernail toward the grass. "Go wipe."

Boy, oh boy, oh boy. She had known Salt since she and Ham were three years old and the three of them had learned their shapes and colors at Miss Agy's nursery school. Salt's parents and her parents were best friends. Honestly, she had a real soft spot for the guy even though he was short and fat and a dope about those dragons. The antimatter of popular in Spratt. But she wasn't shallow, no sir. Salt was basically a member of the family. That's why she cared. That's why she tried.

Plus, it was soothing, nagging Salt. It made her forget that she was maybe standing on the slippery slope of weeniehood herself.

"C'mon Salt, get with it. We go through this every morning. We get off the bus together, thus we *reflect* on each other. Think how you're making me look."

"Sorry," said Salt.

Candi grimaced. *Sorry* didn't cut it. He should work harder at how he looked. Looking good was crucial— why didn't Salt get that?

"But I was shoveling out the camel barns."

"I knew it!" cried Candi. "You promised me you'd stop shoveling manure before school! You *promised*!"

Salt shrugged. "I forgot."

"How 'bout me, Birdbrain? Am I good enough to get off the bus with you?" said Ham.

"Shut up," said Candi absently, watching Salt walk over to the grass by the side of the road and scrape the crud off his boots. Salt looked up.

"What do you think, Candi? Should I tuck my shirt in or leave it out?"

Candi buried her face in her hands and moaned. "Leave it out, Salt. Please. I beg of you."

Frankly, the bus came not a moment too soon.

Later that day in science, the last period of the day, Candi gave the forbidden wad of gum in her mouth two fast, hard, secret chews. She watched Mr. Eggebean walk between the rows, slapping a copy of the midterm facedown on every desk. This was it. Half the grade for evolutionary biology.

Candi glanced at Allison Fishbinder, sitting one seat up and two rows over. Allison, the most popular girl in Spratt and Candi's best friend since forever, was nervously twiddling with the silky-smooth tips of her shining blond hair. Candi fluffed out her bangs and tried to look like she was nervously twiddling too.

It was an effort. Cell structure and basic genetics were easy. And Mr. Eggebean made up the dumbest tests. Multiple choice, true-false, and two essay questions every time. Honestly, why did he even bother?

Allison glanced over. Her face was pale. Candi smiled weakly at Allison, wondering if her own face looked pale, too. Probably not. She felt just fine.

Mr. Eggebean put a test on her desk. He leaned back, a big, pie-eating grin on his face.

"Of course, I always enjoy the little jokes from one of my prize pupils, Candace," cooed Mr. Eggebean. "But I'd like to include your test with the paper I'm writing on the gifted female science student for my master's degree. So could you just answer the questions, please? No backward writing, no mirror writing, no knock-knock jokes about the scientific method written in the margins. Oh, and no quadratic doodling, okay? Since we both know you'll be the first to finish the test, I brought in some of my old copies of *Science and Nature*. There's a terrific article on osmosis in the January issue."

Candi's heart sank. Every single kid in the room had turned to stare at her in utter disbelief. And Allison was glaring at her, the same glare she trained on particularly smart, particularly obnoxious classroom weenies.

Uh-oh. Think fast.

"Gosh, Mr. Eggebean, that's great!" she chirped even as her knuckles twitched, yearning to bop him one on the nose for blowing her cover like that. "Membrane osmosis is fast replacing electrolysis as the method of choice for unwanted hair removal. Not to mention bikini waxing, whoa. Let's talk about something that needs to be relegated to the medieval torture chamber. So you *bet* I'm going to look into it."

The science teacher patted her shoulder and moved off, slightly puzzled. Candi held her breath. Allison turned around. The class turned around. Everybody flipped over the test and sighed.

Candi flipped over her test and sighed, too. Whew. That was close. *Too* close.

She scanned the first question and chewed secretly for a moment, totally depressed. Science was easy. Math was a snap. History was brainless. What a nightmare.

Honestly, all she craved was the familiar comfort of her second-most-popular status. All she wanted was to hang around with Allison and have a lot of fun in all the crucial areas—makeup and clothes and boys. The fastest way to sink all that was to keep on raising her hand. Taking her books home. Reading osmosis articles, a subject that sounded totally . . . fascinating.

Candi gritted her teeth. Allison would never put up with a weenie for a friend. Look at how she treated Salt, for instance, like he was a cheap brand of greasy eye shadow gumming up her eyelids. If Allison ever got wind of how well Candi was doing in school, how much she was starting to think, it would be—the end.

She had to get a grip, that's all. She had to act cute and perky and slightly dumb all the time, just like always. With a deep, heartfelt sigh for the lost chance at boning up on osmosis, Candi watched Allison read through the first question. Allison's lips moved slowly.

Candi picked up her pencil and scanned the first question. She forced her lips to twitch.

She was done with the midterm in twenty-two minutes flat, but Mr. Eggebean was insane if he thought she could just whip out the January issue of *Science and Nature* and study the biology articles. Allison was still guessing at the multiple choice. Candi had to keep her head bent over her test. Like way, way over.

When the dismissal bell woke her up, her cheek was plastered to her desk with drool. Ew.

Chapter Three

—m—

And so after flying the hills and valleys of her adopted territory for the last time, the matriarch stretched out in front of the wheyr, closed her lidless eyes, and . . . breathed her last. Salt's dad closed the South African pasture to unauthorized personnel. Dr. Zhao advised strict nest isolation until the dragon eggs hatched.

They didn't have long to wait. Under a bright spring moon in early March, nine healthy dragonlings slithered into the world. Salt's dad passed out chocolate cigars to all the animal technicians. Salt's mom sent a letter to the Chinese embassy in Washington. It announced the successful hatching and invited Dr. Zhao to Ohio so that he might examine the first dragonlings born outside of China in over two thousand years. Naturally, the Wilds would pay Dr. Zhao's expenses. Naturally.

Salt grinned. When his mom read that part of the

letter out loud at supper that night, he could hear her molars grinding at the thought of having to pay for a first-class plane ticket.

But the coolest thing was that his dad asked him to help out with the wheyr observations.

"Your mom is getting pretty cranky about staff overtime," he explained, "And the animal techs are whining about getting there by seven A.M. So I thought you and I could trade off and cover it." They were standing in front of the stainless steel examination table in the garage lab, sorting through calipers and finalizing the dragons' growth chart methodology. "I bet Mr. Eggebean would give you extra credit in science for an ongoing project like this. You could bring up that C."

"Mr. Eggebean hates me, Dad." Salt lined up the largest caliper, an otoscope, and the baroscope refractor. "Ever since I refused to dissect an earthworm for evolutionary biology, he thinks I'm a weenie."

His voice trailed off. Salt had a short but extremely satisfying daydream about accepting the Nobel Prize for Zoology. Mr. Eggebean would be there, of course, lurking in the back row of the auditorium, hoping that Salt might thank his old science teacher by name, wishing like heck he'd given his prize-winning pupil a decent grade back in seventh grade. Something in the B range, at least. Maybe even an A minus. Whoa.

"They sure don't give the prize to weenies, Mr. Eggebean," Salt mumbled.

"John?"

"Huh?"

"You say something?"

Salt shook off his happy dream, consulted his list, and added a tape measure to the pile of instruments on the table. "I said I'm not a weenie. I just don't think you have to kill something and cut it open in order to understand it. I mean, you think Dr. Zhao would poke around in a dragon's insides just to see what he could see?"

"Not really."

"Well, there ya go." Salt looked up. "You know what the scary thing was? The only kid who agreed with me about the earthworm was Candi Clarke. She said the formaldehyde was stripping off her nail polish."

His dad grinned. "Sounds like Candi."

Salt opened a drawer under the sink and pulled out nine jumbo-sized stool jars. "I'll collect some dragon droppings so we can check for worms."

"Great," said his dad. "Oh. And I dropped off your roll of film at QuickiePhoto. Double prints. You can send a set to Dr. Zhao." Salt nodded.

The next morning before school, Salt loaded up his tool belt, strapped on his backpack, and biked out to the wheyr for seven A.M. stats and observations.

"Hey, little girl," he crooned to the largest of the nest-mates, a dark gray female with the prominent forward-pointing nostrils characteristic of a fire-breather. She wrapped herself twice around his leg and opened her mouth in a soundless hiss. Her fat egg tooth winked in the early morning sun.

As a newly hatched dragonling, she was nothing to write home about. All of her impressive adult structures—her double row of razor fangs, her side-swiping tail spikes, her shimmering opalescent wing membranes—were several molts away. Right now she looked like a colossal but extremely lumpy rat snake, with a bashed-in snout and bugged-out eyes. A face only a mother could love.

A mother—or a guy like John Salt.

"You are just so—ow!" The dragonling bit Salt.

Tears filled his eyes. "It's okay," Salt assured the dragonling. "I'm not mad. I know you're teething and everything."

Salt pinched the dragon firmly behind the jawbones. The dragon's jaw popped, and Salt extracted his hand. He unwrapped the dragonling from his waist and shooed her away. She slithered toward the pile of bones and scales and tattered remnants of translucent wing membranes near the mouth of the wheyr.

Salt dug the egg tooth out of his bleeding hand and

scrutinized it. Seeing his own blood like that always made him a little woozy. Salt had to close his eyes and breathe deep before he could shake out a specimen bag from a snap pocket on his belt. He labeled it "Egg tooth, dragon 'Queenie' (blood, mine)" and dropped the tooth into the bag. Then he watched the nine dragonlings crunch through the bones of their dead mama.

"Hungry, huh? Tastes good, huh? Boy. Bones, muscle, scales, wings—you guys are eating every single bite. Waste not, want not. Just like Eustace Scrubb in *Voyage of the Dawn Treader*. The young dragon dines on the flesh of the old."

He scribbled a few observations in his notebook. Then he unclipped a tape measure from his tool belt and began measuring dragon snouts. The peaceful satisfaction of large-animal work warmed his bones. Salt began to whistle.

He dug a package of hot dogs out of his backpack and used a hot dog to lure Smokey, the runt, onto the livestock scale his dad had trucked out last week. He slid the bar until the scale balanced, then let out a low whistle of pure admiration. One hundred thirty-five pounds. Boy, only five days old, and you could feel the heft of him already, a dense, heat-generating muscle mass covered by the thin layer of fat that insulated the dragons from both heat and cold. "I like to think of dragons as lukewarm-blooded reptiles," joked Dr. Zhao in his letter.

Salt grinned. That Dr. Zhao. What a great sense of humor, huh? He scratched Smokey's swollen wing buds. Smokey undulated with pleasure, and Salt's grin got wider. A winged reptile. A flying dragon. A miracle.

"We never did find out how your mama got here," murmured Salt to the dragonling, "all the way from China. We think maybe a storm blew her north of the Sea of Okhotsk, where she took a wrong turn at the Arctic Circle and drifted down the Canadian Shield. Maybe she tried out the habitat of a Great Lake or two before she settled on her comfort zone in Ohio. After all, Spratt, Ohio, and Beijing, China, are both at forty degrees latitude. Great theory, huh, Smokey?"

Salt nudged Smokey off the scale. The dragonling curled around Salt's boots and gummed the laces. Then he tried to pull off the boots' shiny steel eyes. The dragonlings were crazy about glittering objects—a throwback to the species's treasure-hoarding days. Blackie, a nice-looking female with three trapezoidal markings transverse across the fourth vertebra, caterpillared over and joined her brother. Aww.

In just a few weeks, the dragons' dull gravel coloring would deepen to sea green and gold; they'd go through a wing molt or two, grow to the length of a stretch limo—boy, these dragons would turn into something definitely worth hanging around with.

Blackie lifted her head and gave Salt a long, level stare from her amber eyes.

"Not that you're not spectacular right now," said Salt hastily. "You're spectacular, all right. Straight out of myth and legend. Mysterious. Great. Totally impressive."

Queenie flicked her tongue over the backs of his hands. Pal slithered up Salt's shoulder and down his arm. Salt staggered under the load.

"I don't know. It's like all my life I've been—oof!—sleepwalking," he said. "Just going through the motions. Feeling a little out of it. I mean—ow!—Mr. Eggebean isn't the only one at school who thinks I'm a weenie. Some of the kids do too. And sure, my parents are great and everything, but they're just parents, you know?"

All nine dragons crawled over his feet, chewed on his boots, tickled his fingers with their forked tongues. "And then you guys come along, and boom! The piece of me that I'd been missing all my life just showed up"—Salt tapped his rib bones—"right here."

He tossed the hot dogs into wide-open mouths. "You guys are the greatest thing that's ever happened to me. So let me–ow!—give you a little advice. Don't start on the zebras. It'll drive Mom insane."

Salt tossed Sunshine the last hot dog and bent to scratch Rascal behind the ear folds. "Sure, hot dogs are okay for a snack. But to grow big, you gotta think big. Think Holstein, guys. Yum, yum. Cows with black-and-white spots sure are good eating, and—"

Salt caught sight of his wristwatch. "Crud! It's way after eight o'clock!" He waded through the pack of dragons rolling and mock-fighting on the grass and ran down the hill to his bike. "You're supposed to bring me good fortune!" he yelled over his shoulder. "Not make me late for school!"

Salt pedaled furiously due east, straight across the savannaed plains of the African pasture. He rode north to the tip of the South American marshes and stopped to wash his filthy hands in one of the manmade ponds that housed the roseate spoonbills and the jabirus. He hopped back on his bike, burned rubber across the Asian steppes, opened the timed electronic gate by the Bactrian camel oasis, took a shortcut through old Mr. Slater's fallow cornfield, and bumped onto Route 146 just west of Spratt Grammar. It was a rough, hilly, three-mile bike ride between the wheyr and the school, but Salt made it in record time. He screeched to a halt at the bike rack just inside the school yard. The tardy bell rang.

"Man, oh man, oh man," moaned Salt as he beat it up the stairs. "One more tardy and I'm dead meat!"

But the dragons *had* brought him a little luck, because when he dashed into homeroom, Ms. Jenkins was nowhere to be seen. Kids were draped over their seats, yakking away. A regular Wednesday morning.

The minute they spotted Salt, though, the girls jumped up and began scooching their desks as far away from his—third row, last seat—as they could. Kathi O'Dell threw open all the windows. Missi Wyatt plugged in the box fan sitting on the floor by Ms. Jenkins's desk and turned it on high.

"Hey, wait a minute," Salt protested. "I washed my hands this time." He stuck them out, still damp, palms up. "See?"

"It's not your *hands*, Salt," said Allison Fishbinder from across the room. She cleared her throat and waited until she had everyone's attention. "It's your *hair*. It's your *shirt*. It's your *shoes*. You're gonna stink up the whole *day*. Yuck."

Salt's heart thumped as he basked in the glow of Allison's lovely blue stare. Gosh, Allison was so terrific, huh? So nice and natural, talking to him like that. She talked to him a lot, actually. Like just last week, after Salt had looked deeply and sincerely into her eyes and murmured, "Is this your compact mirror? Because I

34

found it on the floor by the pencil sharpener," Allison had said, "Um. Thanks, Salt."

Um. Thanks, Salt. Wow. Just—*wow.*

Salt knew he wasn't popular. He was kind of husky, kind of slow, and way too easygoing about losing to fit in well at his sports-crazy school. And the stuff that still interested him deeply—bugs and snakes and flying dragons—most kids had left behind in fourth grade.

It bothered him, of course, feeling kind of out of it— but not enough to reach for a scalpel in biology class and go out for the baseball team. Besides, he *liked* spending his lunch recess identifying the bugs that first graders brought over to him on the playground. It was important work, entomology. Plus he made sure the little kids let the bugs go when the bell rang, so he couldn't just stop because a couple of kids thought he was a weenie.

And anyway, Allison Fishbinder, the most popular girl at Spratt, never said a word. She just breezed by him on the playground like it was the most natural thing in the world: John Salt surrounded by bugs.

Salt really admired that.

Ham Clarke came over. "Aw, blow the girls off, Salt," he said. "Dragonstink ain't that bad."

Ham looked at Allison and Candi standing by the

windows. They were fanning themselves with notebooks and complaining at the tops of their lungs. "Allison and Birdbrain make a big deal out of everything. You'd think they'd just learn to hold their pointy little noses and shut up already."

Chapter Four

—‰—

"That test was soooo haaaard," complained Allison Fishbinder as the seventh grade gang all stood in the cafeteria line. "Ms. Jenkins does it just to be mean."

"She gets those tests straight out of the back of college textbooks," said Missi Wyatt. "My cousin goes to Ohio State, and he *swears* he saw Old Lady Jenkins in the copy center with the freshman English textbook."

"Oh, right. Like even a college guy could get a B on that thing," said Ami Orchard-Hill.

"My mom's gonna kill me for flunking," moaned Marianne Mitchell.

"Oh yeah? Well, Coach Bard said he was gonna put me on the bench for the entire softball season if I don't do something about my English grade," announced Kathi O'Dell.

Every single seventh grade girl groaned. Kathi was

their shortstop. They'd never make it to state without her.

"How'd *you* do, Candi?" asked Allison. "You had your head down the whole time."

"Uh. I had to keep my head down because . . . because . . ." Candi chewed thoughtfully. "Oh! I know! Because I was afraid I was gonna bust into tears!"

Wow. What a relief, saying the right thing. All the girls around her nodded sympathetically. Allison patted her shoulder. "Well, you gotta stay out of trouble too," said Allison. "We won't make it to state without our starting pitcher, either." She stopped patting. "Not that I wouldn't like to try out for your pitching slot," she murmured.

Boy, Allison Fishbinder as the opener—they'd be at the bottom of the league in a week flat. Candi shook off her disloyal thought, picked up a tray of lunch glop, and slid it along the lunch line rails. Time to change the subject.

"Okay, Allison, confess. What's up with your makeup?"

Allison smiled happily. "Last week my mom *finally* says, 'Okay, okay. Maybe the dermatologist is right and you do need to use a good brand of hypoallergenic cosmetics.' Gosh, I never thought I'd be thankful for sensitive skin, but as of this week, I am totally mail-order on makeup."

"That's great!" cried Candi, still sliding. She grabbed two milks. "I'm soooo jealous. So what are you buying?"

"Jeez, what do you think? Orléans, stupid."

"I knew it! I knew it! I'd recognize the Orléans skin tones anywhere! They're the best. Their spring line of moisturizing lipsticks and eye shadow colors are absolutely amazing."

"Uh-huh. I got the *plume de Voltaire* lip gloss on back order."

"That'll be a dollar sixty-five, ladies," said the cashier. "Each."

They dug around in their purses.

"Know what's weird?" said Candi. "John Salt's aunt is the director of Orléans Cosmetics Research and Development. She works out of their world headquarters in Paris, France. I saw a picture of her office in last month's *Makeup from the Edge*. It has a view of the Eiffel Tower. Her office, I mean." She popped her gum. "Paris. France. Can you imagine?"

"Buck sixty-five," repeated the cashier. "Let's shake it, ladies. You're holding up the line."

Candi handed the cashier a dollar sixty-five all in dimes. And one nickel. The cashier gave her the evil eye, but Candi ignored her.

"Boy, I'd like to live in Paris," she said, a faraway look in her eyes. "Like Dr. Mary Athena Salt. Did you know she grew up right here in Spratt? Isn't that cool? She's really just the latest example of American expatriates, people who've found real meaning in their lives by moving to France—people like Gertrude Stein and Ernest Hemingway, and—" She broke off at Allison's stare of utter disbelief.

"I can't believe you know somebody named Gertrude," said Allison. "Ew. And what's an expatriate, anyway?"

Uh-oh. Time to really change the subject. "So, didja hear what we're doing in gym this afternoon? Square dancing, can you believe it? Talk about gross."

But Allison didn't want to talk about square dancing, worse luck. "I bet Salt's aunt has a boring job," said Allison as they moved among the lunch tables. "Research, yuck. Pouring stuff into test tubes and pouring stuff out of test tubes. Personally, I'd rather be a runway model."

Candi shut up. All that color preparation and test tube mixing sounded totally fascinating, but no way was she going to admit it. Still, it would be amazing, wouldn't it, to actually *create* your own makeup and not just follow somebody else's idea of the hot new spring colors? Dreamily, she followed Allison toward the back of the cafeteria where the popular kids sat.

So lost in thought was she that Candi almost missed the mention of her personal hero's name.

"Nah," Salt was saying to Ham. Ham, the best baseball

player in Spratt, could have sat in the back too, but for some weird reason he always hung out with Salt at the weenie table near the middle of the room. Her left elbow passed directly over their heads as she breezed by. "I can't. Not this Saturday. My aunt Mary Athena is coming for a visit, and Dad's planning this big welcome-home supper."

Candi stopped dead in her tracks. "Dr. Mary Athena Salt is coming to Spratt?" she screeched. Allison, three feet ahead of her, turned around in surprise.

"I'll be right there," Candi called. "I gotta talk to Ham a minute."

She turned eagerly to Salt—and caught a whiff of dragonstink. Boy, oh boy, oh boy. She tried to breathe through her mouth and talk at the same time.

"Dr. Sald is gonna be in down?" she repeated. "For real? I can'd believe id!"

"Yep," said Salt. "She hasn't been back to Spratt since I was three years old. It was a surprise when she called last night."

"So believe it, Birdbrain," grumbled Ham. "And go sit someplace else."

Candi made sure to whack Ham a good one on the back of his head with the edge of her tray as she walked off, grinning. She floated, practically, to the back of the room and slid into the seat Allison had saved for her.

"Guess what!" she cried. "Dr. Salt—*the* Dr. Salt—is coming to Spratt!"

"Yeah?" said Allison indifferently. "She gonna hand out free makeup samples, you think?"

Candi was stunned. Free makeup samples. Like that was the point?

No. The point was, she had a chance to meet her hero at last—Dr. Mary Athena Salt, the woman who had developed the most wonderful makeup on the planet. The point was, she had a chance to meet Dr. Salt, who had grown up in small-town Ohio and made it all the way to the big time in Paris, France. The point was, she had a chance to meet Dr. Salt, who might possibly be looking for an eager young assistant to take back to Paris, France, for the summer—just in time for June and the big cosmetics show held every year at the Institut des Beaux Visages—whoa. Now that was the point. Boy, oh boy, oh boy.

Candi toyed with her glop, thinking hard. She had to meet Dr. Salt, she just had to. But how? Hmm.

Her eyes popped open. "Allison and me could just happen to bike over to Salt's house and drop off a plate of Mom's cookies," she murmured. "Like a total coincidence." She turned to Allison, her eyes shining, full of her brilliant plan.

"Allison!" she cried. "I have this great idea!"

"Yeah?"

"This Saturday, let's bike over to Salt's house—"

"Salt? You mean John Salt? Why in the world would I want to go over to his house?"

"No, listen! And sort of introduce ourselves to his—"

"Sorry, Candi. My mom is taking me to Columbus for spring clothes shopping. We'll probably hit Nordstrom's and everything, ya know?"

"Oh. Right. Sure." Candi swallowed hard. Well, shoot. She'd have to ask around, find somebody who wasn't busy. Popular people never went anywhere alone. It was the rule. If you went someplace alone, it looked like you didn't have anybody to share your interests with or something. And nothing could be further from the truth, of course.

Well, it was kind of last minute, but she'd dig up somebody, and then boy, oh boy, oh boy! Meeting Dr. Mary Athena Salt in person and shaking that great woman's hand! Candi sighed with satisfaction.

Allison looked up at the clock. "Gosh, lunch is almost over," she said. "And we have to go to gym next." She turned to Candi. "I hear we're square dancing. Talk about gross."

Chapter Five

—∿∿—

The cow mooed contentedly as she ambled toward the
fresh hay flake. She lifted her head, still chewing, and
watched Salt stow the hay fork on a rack inside the shed
and close the door. Salt walked over to a large tree a
hundred yards away and leaned against the trunk. He
took the lens caps off his binoculars. He was all set.

From the cow's point of view, Salt supposed, things
couldn't be better. She certainly had been easy to cut
out of the herd at the Holstein corral on the other end
of the South African pasture. Salt had tugged once on
her ear, and she had followed him docilely through the
gate and down the dirt track winding between the hills.
Genetic memories of Swiss alpine meadows imprinted
on her bovine brain must have made the bright blue
sky, the warm sun, and the guiding tug on her ear all
sweetly familiar.

And boy howdy, the field the boy had brought her to was great, just great. A wide-open tallgrass meadow dotted with trees and early-spring flowers and a flake of hay—pure cow heaven. She'd eat her fill and then lie down in a sunny spot and chew cud. Maybe doze off. She was safe as cow stalls here. Aside from the motionless boy and a large, black bird circling high overhead, there was not another living thing in sight. Perfect.

The wind blew softly. The cow teased the hay apart with her lips and grazed on.

Had the Holstein bothered to look up, she would have noticed the jerky descent of the bird. As it spiraled lower, she might have wondered why the bird, a common red-necked turkey buzzard, had a large, white patch of surgical gauze taped over its left eye. The bird sailed toward Salt's tree, aiming for the top branch. It undershot the branch and crashed into a limb three feet above Salt's head. The buzzard grabbed a foothold, lost its grip, and spun halfway around the branch before yanking itself upright. A rusty black tail feather floated onto Salt's shoulder.

"Hey, Loretta, how's the pretty girl," murmured Salt. "Won't be long, now. See? Queenie's moving the pack. Forty yards away and closing in." He held the binoculars up to his eyes.

Queenie's head periscoped over the long grass just

45

beginning to green with spring. Her tongue flicked in and out, smelling the air.

According to Dr. Zhao's letter, after the dragonlings went through the primary wing molt, the wheyr's alpha female could be identified by the crimson markings on her "tiger's paw"—the five-toed bird's-foot that formed the apex of a dragon's wing. As Queenie considered the cow, her claws flexed. First the right foot, then the left. Through the binoculars, Salt watched Queenie's claws extend and retract. The flash of her bloodred underpaws made him grin. Queenie had emerged as the wheyr's alpha female. Totally cool. Queenie was one smart cookie.

Her head disappeared from sight. Faint rustling that might be nothing more than the wind playing in the grass circled the Holstein. Head down, unsuspecting, the cow continued to graze.

The Holstein still had all the advantages of size and speed, of course. For the dragonlings were just babies, really, much slower and clumsier than the cow. And while their juvenile coloration provided effective camouflage, their wings were not quite half grown and only partially opened. Aerial attack, the preferred hunting method of mature dragons, was out of the question.

"So they're gonna have to stalk her," Salt said to Loretta. The grass rustled. The circle tightened.

Salt shook his head in admiration. Dragons sure were sneaky things, either lying low in the grass or soaring high among the clouds. No wonder dragons had been nothing more than fantastic creatures of myth and legend until that summer ten years ago, when Dr. Zhao began to roam the vast, stony wastelands of western China, field researching the nearly extinct dwarf yak.

Late one evening Dr. Zhao built his tent shelter halfway up the slope of a chain of hills overlooking a lake. At dawn a fully mature dragon rose silently out of a hidden wheyr, downwind and ten yards east of his shelter. As Dr. Zhao later wrote in his groundbreaking essay "*Drago Orientis* of Western China," published in *Science and Nature*, this dragon was so swiftly gone behind the clouds that Dr. Zhao never actually saw what hit him, though the resulting windstorm nearly blew him and his shelter back to Ürümqi. Since it was hardly the place for tornados, the rumpled zoologist began to look around.

"Surely," wrote Dr. Zhao, "those odd scarpa formations had been undercut by the constant rub of something very large and heavy. Surely that three-foot-wide scrap of scale molt (silky green opalescence, so delicate looking, yet so tough that my pocketknife scarcely nicked the surface) that I found wedged between two rocks belonged to no reptile of my knowledge. And surely, surely, the closer I got to the creature's ingeniously hidden lair, the greater the carnivorous stench. Clearly I had stumbled upon a tremendously large and hungry factor in the near-extinction of the dwarf yak. But what, exactly, had I found?"

Three days later Dr. Zhao encountered his second dragon, a juvenile on its first flight. "A most holy moment," wrote Dr. Zhao with typical insight. "Truly I was at one with the universe."

Salt smiled fondly, remembering how Allison Fishbinder had been one with the universe too, at her first sight of a flying dragon. A couple of weeks after the matriarch had settled at the Wilds, the dragon had dive-bombed the school's outdoor basketball courts during lunch, mildly curious, perhaps, about this pack of inedible human beings jumping around outside and screeching. Allison happened to stroll out of the cafeteria doors just as the dragon turned a loop-the-loop over the baseball field and made another overhead pass.

"So that's the dragon, huh?" Allison had said. "Wow."

"She said *wow* like she really meant it," Salt murmured to Loretta as he watched the Holstein graze. "Just—*wow*. You know?"

The wind died down. The Holstein jerked her head and mooed, suspicious, finally, at the soft rustling all around her. Her sudden movement in his direction spooked poor Smokey. He squeaked in fright, turned tail, and slithered away. Rascal lost his nerve too.

The rest of the dragonlings milled around, trying to regroup. The Holstein pawed the ground, then lowered her head and charged. The left flank, led by Sparky, the alpha male, held firm. Trigger and Blackie broke cover, reared up, and spat at the charging cow. The sight of three extremely large, hissing snakes in the grass made the Holstein reconsider her headlong charge. She veered to the right.

Rusty and Pal undulated toward her, but they weren't fast enough to stop her. The Holstein, still bucking and snorting, zigged right, zagged left, then broke into a jog trot for the home corral.

Salt shook his head sadly. They'd never catch her now.

Up popped Queenie, two inches under the cow's nose, her mouth wide open in a pint-sized dragonic bellow. The cow got an intimate look at the double row of razor-edged incisors erupting from the dragonling's gums; the quivering forked tongue; the deep red tunnel of the segmented, flexible gullet ready to swallow a large chunk of cow. The Holstein jumped sideways in sheer surprise—straight into Sunshine's waiting jaws.

"Wow," said Salt to Loretta. "Just—wow. A successful hunt nine days after hatching. We have an extremely intuitive dragon pack here. Dr. Zhao says the first kill usually happens two weeks after hatching. I can't wait to write him."

He set the binoculars on the ground by his foot and wrote up his observations in his notebook. He sketched out the dragonlings' stalk formation using football x's and o's. Loretta trained her good eye on the feeding dragons. She took off, airplaning low over his head, and crash-landed awkwardly on the cow carcass runway.

Salt biked home. Ham Clarke was waiting for him in the backyard, leaning against the white-on-red State Game Refuge/Trespassing Unlawful sign posted next to the barbed-wire fence that separated the Salts' driveway from one of the Wilds' East African pastures. A greater kudu and a couple of sable antelope had wandered over. Ham was scratching the kudu's back with a stick.

"Hey, Salt," said Ham. "Nobody home."

"Nah. They just didn't hear you knock, I bet," said Salt. "My aunt's gonna be here any minute. Dad's sucking up to Mom because he's trying to get her to fund six zebras. She said she'd think about it, so he's been cooking and cleaning all afternoon. Mom's on the phone with some work crisis."

They climbed the back stairs and passed a meshed aviary that enclosed the far end of the porch.

"Got another buzzard, huh?" asked Ham, looking at

the fresh bone pile in the bottom of the cage.

"Uh-huh," said Salt. "I named her Loretta. Uncle Dinsmore told me that was the name of his girlfriend in high school." He opened the aviary door. "She'll be back when she's done scavenging the dragonlings' kill."

They walked into the kitchen. It smelled of citron and cardamom and cleanser. Salt wrinkled his nose. "Hey, Dad!" he yelled up the stairs. "Can Ham stay for supper?"

"Not that you'd want to," he told Ham. "Dad's been cooking straight out of *The Tightwad Gourmet* again. Everything's gonna taste like Hungarian pepper."

Salt stopped. His mom swept down the stairs and stormed through the kitchen. Her left hand yanked at the collar of her legislators suit—a steel gray power suit with a eighteen-karat-gold circle pin stabbed through the lapel—as her right hand swung a bulging black briefcase. She stormed to the back door, turned, and stared the boys down.

"Those . . . lawmakers," she sneered, "up in Columbus have seen fit to pull the funding for our Ethiopian wolf breeding program. Ten o'clock last night in special session." She patted the inside pocket of her silk-lined suit, where she kept her betel-nut rosary and a wad of business cards.

"Uh-oh," said Salt.

Gone was the mom in fuzzy pink slippers who cried

51

at old movies about sinking ships. Gone was the able administrator, the dedicated fund-raiser, the brilliant director of a multimillion-dollar nonprofit animal refuge. This was feral mom, berserker mom, the mom whose helpless babies were being menaced by a pack of howling legislators ravenous for funding cuts. It didn't matter that the helpless babies were four scrawny, bad-tempered wolves that dug holes under the East African enclosure and chased ostriches for fun. Nope. Those were *her* wolves, *her* breeding program, and when his mom got her funding cut—watch out.

"*Uh-oh* is right!" roared his mom. "*Uh-oh* is finding out the General Assembly plans another special session tonight! Who knows what those so-called representatives will defund next if I'm not there to fight it!"

Salt's heart sank. Sure, he'd been through this a hundred times before, but that didn't make it any easier. His mom would drop everything until the wolf program was back on line. His dad would drop everything until the wolf program was back on line. Which meant that Salt was in for a boatload of work until the wolf program was back on line. Cooking. Laundry. Cutting the grass. Of course Salt was disturbed about the funding cuts. Of course. He was just sorry about getting stuck with all the housework for the foreseeable future. He had a small, sad picture of a silent TV covered in dust; a ball and chain and a sinkful of dirty dishes; a poor semi-orphaned boy too exhausted by the flood of chores to call Allison about the seventh grade dance.

"Gosh, Mom, I really hate to see you go," said Salt feelingly as his dad loped down the stairs. He was wearing his Ohio State alumni necktie and his one and only suit coat. Salt gave him a look.

"Don't worry, John, I'm going with her," his dad said. "I'll keep an eye on her."

"Uh. Dad? That's what you said last time."

"Yeah. Boy. That was embarrassing, wasn't it? Well, I just won't let her get close enough to the governor to throw a punch this time."

Salt's mom ran bright pink lipstick over and over her mouth. "I'm telling you, they even think about cutting the funds for the renovations to the South American habitats, there's gonna be legislative *blood* all over the statehouse *floor*!"

Salt's dad steered her out the door. "You betcha, SueAnn. We're gonna fight 'em tooth and nail. But first we're gonna get in the Jeep and drive with all the windows rolled down so we cool off a little before we talk to any legislators."

Salt and Ham followed them onto the back porch. "Uh, Dad? What about Aunt Mary Athena?"

"Oh, right." His dad squinted thoughtfully at Loretta's

bone pile. "Well, I'm sure she'll understand. Besides, supper's all ready. All you have to do is dish it out and clean up afterward. Your aunt won't be any trouble. She's a great old gal. You'll see."

Ham leaned over the porch rail and pointed up the driveway. "You can tell her good-bye yourself, Mr. Salt. Because here she comes."

A cherry red Range Rover with rental plates gunned up the driveway. It swerved past the barbed-wire fence, sprayed the Salts' Jeep with gravel, and came to a screeching halt behind the pickup, missing the back fender by half an inch.

Salt watched the Rover's door open. So this was his aunt Mary Athena, whom he hadn't seen since he was three years old. Aunt Mary Athena was a couple of years older than his dad, which made her pretty old. Almost fifty. He'd always imagined her as his jolly old aunt—somebody like the plump, wrinkly ladies at nine-o'clock Mass, cheerfully flaking face powder in the pews and bestowing lipsticky Sunday smiles on him during the passing of the peace.

But the aunt who got out of the Rover was skinny as a toothpick, dressed entirely in black except for a white leather belt slung low around her bony hips. The belt had a whole bunch of snaps and grommets and loops and an oversized metal buckle. It would make a great

54

utility belt. The loops looked sturdy enough to hold a pickaxe, but from the way his mom was casting little yearning glances, Salt was pretty sure his aunt's belt was more cutting-edge fashion accessory than functional tool holder.

Salt scratched his head, puzzled. And nobody had hair that color on purpose, did they? That ultrashiny metallic red, cut short and slicked into place by a ton of hair stuff?

Her skin—looking flawless and pale—caught the light as she stepped away from the shade trees near the drive and into a patch of golden afternoon sun. Aunt Mary Athena blinked and squinted and glanced nervously around, like somebody who hadn't been outside in the fresh air for a while. Her blinking gaze fell on the group gathered on the back porch. She stopped, drew herself up, and threw out her arms as if to embrace them all. For some reason, it made Salt shiver.

"My darling family!" she cried in a surprisingly deep voice for such a skinny toothpick. "I've come home!"

She glided up the stairs. "Peter, little brother," she murmured, grabbing Salt's dad by his elbows and pinning them to his side. She maneuvered her face within eight inches of his cheek and planted an air kiss, one on each side, very French.

"Hey, Spud," said Salt's dad, struggling to free his

arms so he could hug her, "it's great to see you."

Aunt Mary Athena winced. "Oh dear," she murmured. "One never outgrows one's awful childhood nickname with one's family, does one?"

She turned his dad loose, slid out of hugging range, and grabbed his mom. "And SueAnn, what a darling suit! You look precious!" she cooed.

Frankly, standing next to the polished, elegant figure of Aunt Mary Athena, Salt's tall, athletic mom looked like a goodish chunk of midwestern pole barn. "Are those shoulder pads? How divinely retro."

She glided toward Ham. "My, how you've grown, John." She grabbed Ham's elbows. "What happened to those chubby little cheeks I remember so well?"

"They're right over there," said Ham, dodging Aunt Mary Athena's air kiss. "I'm Cheeks's friend." Salt smiled weakly at his aunt as she pounced.

"Ah. How unobservant of me. I should have recognized those chipmunk cheeks." She air kissed one chipmunk. "You're the spitting image of your . . . roly-poly . . . Uncle Dinsmore."

The air got kissed again. Up close you could see a lot of what Aunt Mary Athena was trying to hide: crows'-feet around her eyes, wrinkles around her mouth, the sag in her jawline that was turning into what would someday be two nice-sized jowls. Up close she looked weird and scary, both. Even worse, Salt had the sneaking suspicion that his aunt had been a nanosecond away from calling Great-uncle Dinsmore *fat*.

He tried to set the record straight. "Uncle Dinsmore isn't fa—roly-poly, Aunt Mary Athena. He just has big bones from being a plumber all his life."

He was sure he heard her sniff disdainfully, but when he looked at her, she was all twinkly smiles.

"Well," Aunt Mary Athena said, "aren't you going to invite me in?"

All those air kisses had rubbed a smear of deep red lipstick onto her right incisor. It glistened like a small drop of blood against the perfect whiteness of her teeth. Salt frowned. She didn't look like his aunt. She didn't look like anybody's aunt. She gave Salt a funny feeling.

"Oh, right," said Salt's dad, running his fingers through his hair until it stood up every which way. "Listen Spud, SueAnn and I have to drop everything and drive to Columbus this evening."

Aunt Mary Athena's eyes opened in surprise. "Columbus? Columbus, Ohio? Whyever would you voluntarily spend an evening in Columbus?"

"Because," roared Salt's mom, forgetting her fashion-accessory envy and getting mad all over again, "those low-down, good-for-nothing, bloodsucking, two-timing *legislators* cut my *wolf funding*!"

His aunt threw up her hands in horror. "No!"

"Yes!"

"Oh no!"

"Oh *yes*! And you better believe they're gonna try to axe the rhino insemination program next!"

"Dear, oh dear. This is so upsetting," soothed Aunt Mary Athena. She linked arms with Salt's mom and guided her to the passenger side of the Jeep. "How despicable. Of course you must go and salvage what you can. Believe me, if there's one thing I understand, it's a work crisis."

Salt's mom got in and buckled her seat belt. "Well, gosh, Mary Athena, you're just as nice as you can be. Thanks for being so good about this. We'll be back as soon as we can. In the meantime, John can show you around." She yelled out the Jeep's window at Salt. "Sweetie! Show your aunt around!"

Salt smiled weakly.

Salt's dad loped down the back porch stairs. He frowned at the grass. "John, weren't you supposed to mow the lawn before your aunt got here?"

"Jeez, Dad, Mom was on the phone in the kitchen all afternoon, and the mower's real noisy."

His aunt stood back against the trees by the barbed-wire fence and laughed a trilling little laugh. "I recall a certain younger brother of mine weaseling out of lawn duty every chance he got."

Salt looked at his aunt. Maybe he could learn to like her after all.

"Yeah, so it's a genetic marker," grumbled his dad as he got behind the wheel. "An allergy to push-mower handles. We all have to learn to rise above our chromosomes. So tomorrow without fail, John. Got it?"

"Sure, Dad," murmured Salt as he waved good-bye, "sure, sure, sure." Ham punched his shoulder and grinned.

As the Jeep backed out of the driveway, Candi Clarke came coasting up the gravel on her bike. She had one hand on the handlebars and the other on a tinfoil-covered plate. She swerved around the Jeep, bumped over the grass, and ditched her bike by the garage. She waved to the Jeep.

"'Bye, Mr. Salt! 'Bye, Mrs. Salt! Have fun!" she yelled. She looked up at Salt, still on the porch. "So they going on a date or something, all dressed up like that?"

"What're *you* doing here, Birdbrain?" grumbled Ham. "And where's your pack of stupid friends?"

Candi paused, her hand hovering over the plate. "Oh. Right. Well, listen, Ham, if anybody asks, you made me come here with you."

She peeled back a corner of the tinfoil. "Mom baked today," she said. The delicious smell of warm chocolate and coconut drifted up the stairs. Salt's mouth filled with drool. "A double batch of chunky chocolate chew-chews. They're for your aunt, to welcome her back to Spratt." Candi looked around eagerly. "So where is she?"

Aunt Mary Athena stepped out of the shadow of the trees. Candi gave a little scream of pure delight.

"Well, *hi*, Dr. Salt! I'm Candi Clarke, and I sure am glad to meet you!" She charged across the driveway, tore off the tinfoil, and thrust out the plate. "Mom just took 'em out of the oven!"

Aunt Mary Athena eyeballed the plate. She picked up the smallest chew-chew and held it up between thumb and forefinger. "A mother who bakes. How wonderfully quaint."

Her twinkly smile held the faintest of sneers. At least Salt thought it was a sneer. He checked to see if the Clarke kids caught it, but they were both grinning like maniacs, proud of their mom's cooking. He must be imagining it.

His aunt, still smiling, dropped the chew onto the plate and dusted her fingertips. "Tell me, John—"

She broke off with a screech and threw her arms over her head as Loretta swooped low over the treetops toward the porch, coming in for a landing. The buzzard flew through the open cage door, missed the perch, and crashed into the chicken wire at the end of the cage. She staggered to her feet and shook her rumpled feathers into place. Salt closed the aviary door.

His aunt climbed the stairs, Candi crowding close behind, and stared at Loretta. "Good grief, is that thing a *bird*?" She pinched her nose shut and took a quick step backward, nearly shoving Candi off the porch. "How can a bird smell so rank?"

Salt's funny feeling about his aunt grew. She made it sound like Loretta's odor was a bad thing. But Loretta was a carrion eater. Successful carrion eaters were *supposed* to smell rank. That's how you knew they were holding up their end of the ecosystem.

On the other hand, Aunt Mary Athena, born and raised a country girl, had beat it out of Spratt and into the big city the minute she could. She'd probably hadn't thought about buzzards in years. After all, she worked in makeup, where appearance is everything. Buzzards weren't big on personal grooming.

So he'd have to cut her some slack. Be nice to her even if she had been rude and insensitive about Loretta. Salt pushed aside the funny little feeling and said politely, "Well, this smell isn't too bad, Aunt Mary Athena. Honest, you should get a whiff after she's gotten hold of a skunk."

He grabbed a chew that was about to fall off the edge of Candi's plate and popped it into his mouth. "Dad found her in the dragons' pasture with a BB pellet straight through her eye. The stitches come out in a couple of days." He swallowed. "She sure loves those dragons. Flies out to the wheyr every chance she gets."

"Oh my, the dragons, yes," murmured Aunt Mary Athena, her fingers still over her nose. "Tell me about the dragons."

Salt patted the aviary door fondly. "Well, me and Loretta sure were proud of 'em today, weren't we, pretty girl? The dragonlings pulled down their first cow. It was great."

He light-fingered a couple more chews. "Saaaalt," said Candi warningly. "These are for your aunt."

"It's quite all right by me," said Aunt Mary Athena. "I'm not fond of coconut." With an effort she pulled her hand away from her face. "And chocolate makes one's face go all podgy."

She stroked her chin with the backs of her fingers, checking for podginess, whatever that was. "Why don't you and your little friends do me a great, big favor and fetch my suitcases from the Rover, hmm? And *do* be careful with the three smaller ones." She smiled a twinkly smile. "My cosmetics bags."

When the three of them—a suitcase in each hand, a garment bag slung bandolier style over Ham's back, and a shiny blue Tiffany's shopping bag clamped between

Candi's teeth—managed to lumber up the back stairs and waddle into the kitchen, they found Aunt Mary Athena standing in front of an appetizer tray of veggies and dip, a look of pain on her face.

"That clam dip contains real sour cream, doesn't it?" she asked, more in sorrow than in anger. "And the carrot sticks are absolutely huge."

"Yep," said Salt, hitching up the suitcases and trying not to look like he was about to drop everything, "Dad spent the whole day cooking. There's a salad in the fridge and a casserole and garlic bread in the oven."

"Ah. I'd forgotten how midwesterners eat and eat," his aunt murmured. "A shame, really."

But Candi had a brilliant idea. She dropped the suitcases, spat out the Tiffany's bag, and hurried to the oven.

"Gosh, Dr. Salt's right," she exclaimed, peering at the sea of tinfoil-wrapped objects warming in the oven. "There's way too much food for just the two of you."

She straightened up. "And with four places set at the table, me and Ham might as well stay for supper, huh?"

Chapter Six

—◆—

Candi Clarke galloped happily between the oven and refrigerator in the Salts' kitchen. Boy, oh boy, oh boy. Sometimes it just happens. All the way over on her bike, she had been hoping for an invitation to supper. Too bad about Mrs. Salt and the funding cuts and all, but boy, oh boy, oh boy.

"Okay. Get psyched," she murmured as she hip-bumped the fridge shut and danced through the doorway into the dining room. She lit the candles on table. "Me, sitting next to Dr. Salt at the table. Me, amazing her with my total grasp of the cosmetic color industry. Me, asking Dr. Salt . . ."

She trailed off, looking doubtfully at the spinach–and–farmer cheese soufflé, the clam dip, the bowl of Hungarian pepper pears. "Jeez, who'd want to eat this stuff?" she muttered. "Good thing Mom baked today."

"Hey, everybody!" she yelled into the living room, where Salt, Ham, and Dr. Salt were sitting around trying to think up stuff to say to one another. "Time to eat!"

"Ah, candlelight. How lovely," said Dr. Salt as she came into the dining room. "We'll just forgo these harsh incandescents." She flicked off the overhead light.

She nudged Salt aside and sat in the chair directly opposite the huge wall mirror above the sideboard. "Candlelight is so appropriate for dining." She stared deeply into the mirror, turning her head from side to side. "Aids digestion and hides all those naughty little wrinkles." She stroked her throat.

"Gosh, me too, Dr. Salt," chirped Candi as she plopped down across from her personal hero and dished out the main course. "Candles are great. So, do you think the trend toward pastel eye colors will last through the summer?"

Candi dug around in her soufflé. Each spinach string made her mouth form a silent *ew*. She scraped the strings off the side of her plate and covered the mess with her napkin. "They're junk, doncha think? I mean, like mint green is supposed to be a *color*? I wanna see some colors that will really light up my eyeballs. Scarlet! Amber! Cerulean! Know what I mean?"

Candi stopped, slightly embarrassed. Um, maybe Dr. Salt didn't know. After all, Dr. Salt was dressed in a sleek black silk catsuit beneath a sleek black calfskin skirt; the perfect outfit to show off the perfect accessory, a killer gorgeous iTellit grommet belt. Candi's fingers itched to explore its butter smooth leather and squeal about the outrageous price. Boy, oh boy, oh boy, Dr. Salt sure looked glamorous, sitting there surrounded by the green plaid curtains and baby blue walls of the Salts' dining room.

Candi sighed. Okay, she knew she was unworthy. Too young, too inexperienced. She glanced down at her favorite outfit: leather-laced jeans and tight yellow tie-dye. Too colorfully dressed, even—but she'd ask anyway. Because you never know.

"So, Dr. Salt, do you think you could use a real enthusiastic personal assistant while you're here? I mean, Spratt's changed a lot and—"

Dr. Salt raised one eyebrow, amused. "Name one thing that's changed in the last thirty years."

Candi blinked, astonished. "Well . . . lots of things! Lots and lots! Like they built those retirement condos on Rix Mill Road, and the Gundersons remodeled their grocery store, and . . ."

She took a deep breath. Now was not the time to get distracted. She had to concentrate. "What I mean is, Dr. Salt, what I really, really mean from the bottom of my heart, is maybe what you need is a totally dedicated personal assistant who would be happy to assist you all summer long, especially at the Institut des Beaux Visages Vendors Show in"—she took her first deep breath of the evening—"Paris, France."

"Ah, the Paris cosmetics show. And what would you know about that?"

Candi leaned forward eagerly. "I read all about it in the spring issue of *Makeup from the Edge*. All the people who matter in the cosmetic industry show up, and the direction of next year's makeup colors are pretty well decided over glasses of champagne, and—"

"All the people who matter," murmured Dr. Salt. "How right you are, Constance. My extremely promising research into antiaging is going to be the hit of this year's Institut." Dr. Salt fingered her silk sleeve and glanced over Candi's head into the mirror. She stroked her cheek and smiled meltingly at her candlelit reflection.

Candi couldn't take her eyes off Dr. Salt. Jeez, she was so perfect, with flawless makeup and French manicure and boy, that sleek, gleaming hair. Not that she was pretty, exactly. More like . . . amazing looking, which for a woman as old as Dr. Salt was as close to pretty as she was going to get anymore. And smart? Definitely. You couldn't miss the keen intelligence shining out of Dr. Salt's classically defined eyes. Amazing looking, smart . . .

and the hit of the Institut des Beaux Visages. That made her popular, to boot.

Whoa. Bet nobody in Paris, France, stared at Dr. Salt in disbelief every time she made one little offhand remark about Blaise Pascal and his groundbreaking work in probability theories. Bet nobody in Paris, France, thought being a research scientist was dumb. Bet everybody in Paris, France, wore iTellit grommet belts.

Just like Dr. Salt.

Candi's eyes widened. Could it be possible that in addition to being a city of culture, of ideas, of really amazing clothes, Paris, France, was the one place on earth where a girl could be pretty, smart, *and* popular—all at the same time?

Wow. Just—wow. She had to get to Paris. She just had to. The city where all her dreams would come true.

There was, however, just this one tiny problem.

"Um. You're working on a wrinkle creme? Alpha hydroxylase, Retin-A, antioxidants, vitamin E, and all that? Shoot. I'm way more knowledgeable about actual makeup. Oh. And it's Candi. My name is Candi. With an *i*."

"Hmm," said Dr. Salt absently, prodding her fork through the minuscule portion of clam dip on her plate. "Got it." She laid her fork upon her plate, crossed it with her knife, then rose from her chair and glided to the sideboard, where she had left her iTellit grommet handbag. "John, your parents don't happen to drink a really good brand of mineral water?"

"Uh-uh. We drink it straight out of the faucet." Salt paused, his hand hovering over the serving spoon. "Dad has a couple of gallons of distilled water in the garage. Want me to get 'em?"

Candi could have sworn a faint sneer passed over Dr. Salt's face before being replaced by a twinkly smile. "Thank you, but no. I'll just have to swallow these dry."

She held out a fistful of weedy green capsules. "Oat grass and seaweed stems in a water-soluble vitamin base," she explained. "My six o'clock supplements. Good for the skin. Good, but not great. And at my time of life"—Dr. Salt turned to examine her face in the mirror, turning her head from side to side—"*good* just isn't enough anymore."

"You could get a whaddayacall it. A face-lift," said Ham helpfully. "Like movie stars. Bet you can afford it. Ow! Quit kicking me, Birdbrain!"

"Then shut up, stupid," Candi hissed, though to be honest she had been about to say the same thing.

"Ah. Plastic surgery," murmured Dr. Salt. She popped green capsules one by one into her mouth, her neck so slender and swanlike you could watch the pills undulate down her throat. "Chemical peels, collagen implants, Botox injections. The last resort of poor, benighted fools. A *jeune-fille* face fashioned out of old, decrepit skin. You can spot those poor unfortunates across the crowded room of every cocktail party on the planet; legions of dried-up ancients, transparent skin stretched unnaturally across the cheekbones. A death mask. Sometimes, up close you can even see . . . the scars." Dr. Salt closed her eyes, horrified.

"This is why my research is so important." Dr. Salt opened her eyes after a moment. "I yearn to save mankind from the cruelty of the peel, the implant . . . the knife." She shuddered delicately. "I am devoted to the vision of creating an all-natural, biodegradable, rejuvenating wrinkle creme so that we may all enjoy year after ageless year."

She gazed at them as she glided across the room to her chair. "This, my little friends, is my quest. My dream. My *raison d'etre*." She lifted her glass of grape juice into the air and proclaimed, "To life!"

"Gosh, Dr. Salt, count me in!" cried Candi, hopping up and clinking glasses enthusiastically, slopping a little juice on Mrs. Salt's best polyester tablecloth. She glared at Ham and Salt until they hoisted their glasses, too. "We're all right behind you, aren't we, guys?"

"Um, sure," said Salt. It sounded more like a question

than an answer. Candi shot him a dirty look and hoisted her glass higher. "To life!" she announced.

Dr. Salt nodded and smiled and lowered her glass. She took a dainty sip at the rim of the glass. Her lips never quite touched the juice.

"The patent money won't hurt, of course," she murmured as she folded her hands neatly in her lap. She winked charmingly. "The creme ought to be inexpensive to produce once I acquire a steady supply of the main ingredient. And the retail markup will be quite satisfying." A tiny smile played around the corners of her mouth. "But enough about me. Tell me, John, about the dragons."

Salt looked up, his mouth already full of Hungarian pepper pears. He chewed and swallowed. "You're interested in the dragons? Really?"

Dr. Salt stroked her jawline with the backs of her fingers. "Of course. I'm a Salt, aren't I? We Salts have animal research bred into our blood and bones."

Candi put down her glass and frowned. Well, shoot. Wasn't *that* just the total end of a fascinating conversation?

Salt started yakking on and on about those stupid dragons. Completely bored, Candi cleared the table and brought in her mom's chew-chews. She ate one and watched Salt trip over his own feet as he demonstrated how a dragon took off in a headwind; where, precisely, a dragon's olfactory organs were located (ew); why a dragon preferred to hunt in the evening. Salt sure got into those dragons. Ham, too. Course Ham was twelve minutes younger, which made him twelve minutes dumber. Boy, oh boy. Allison was right. Men and their snakes.

She was so bored, she had nothing to do but think about stuff. Frankly, her thoughts were making her nervous. Antiaging. Her personal hero was in Spratt to research antiaging. Antiaging sure wasn't going to get a fresh-faced twelve-year-old on a plane to the cosmetics show in Paris. Brooding, Candi ate a couple more chews. She leaned back and licked her fingers.

When the phone rang, Salt could barely tear himself away to answer it. He dashed into the kitchen and dashed back before Candi could grab Dr. Salt's attention.

"Dad wants to talk to you, Aunt Mary Athena," he said. "The phone's in the kitchen next to the fridge."

"So—your dad say if your mom picked a fight with anybody yet, Salt?" asked Ham as Dr. Salt glided out of the dining room.

"Uh-uh. He's been able to keep his body between her and the legislators so far. But the Assembly's gone into closed doors. Mom and Dad are going to grab a hotel room and wait it out up there."

They listened to the murmur of Dr. Salt's voice from

the kitchen. "My aunt is going to be in charge around here." Salt frowned at the guttering candles, the empty chew-chew plate. He looked like he'd been thinking stuff over too. "She's—I don't know. I get this funny feeling about her."

Candi could hardly believe it. "Are you insane, Salt? You're the luckiest kid on the planet to have an aunt like Dr. Salt! She's smart. She's got the best haircut. And she's gonna be the toast of the cosmetics show. What's to feel funny about?"

Salt scratched his head until the hair around his right ear stuck straight out. "I dunno. There's just something . . . weird about this whole visit."

"Your aunt's okay, Salt," said Ham. "It's those grass seed things she eats that are weird. Bet *you'd* love 'em, huh, Birdbrain?"

"Shut up," said Candi as Dr. Salt came into the room and flicked on the overhead light.

"Our party's over, I'm afraid," she said. "Your mother's tied up with this funding snafu, and your father knows better than to leave her in Columbus without supervision. That leaves you and me, John, to hold down the fort for the next couple of days. Fortunately, your father has offered me the use of his garage lab."

She stopped and tapped her chin with one buffed

and gleaming fingernail. "Perhaps this will work out all the better. I'll make some phone calls to my office for supplies."

She slipped out of the room. "Perhaps your little friends would like to stay and help you with the dishes, John," she said over her shoulder. "I'll be on my cell to Paris. Try not to bang the pots, hmm?"

Chapter Seven

—m—

The next Friday afternoon, Salt came home from school and found his dad in the bedroom, two open suitcases on the bed.

"Great, you're home," said Salt.

"Yup," said his dad. "Just long enough to pack." He gestured at the suitcases. "One for me, one for your mom."

Salt sat down on the edge of the bed. "So how's she doing?"

"Well. Frankly, she didn't take it too well. The funding cuts, I mean," said his dad.

Salt nodded. He understood that, totally. His mom was tall and strong and brave and smart. She was gentle and tenderhearted toward all the Wilds' creatures— even the Mongolian ferrets, which bit. Her tender heart was the main reason she got so hacked when the state legislature monkeyed with the Wilds' funding. Taking food out of her babies' mouths, plus screwing up the quarterly budget. His mom really hated that.

"So now your mom's hooked up with Sarah Hamburg from the National Zoo in D.C. They're going to petition the federal government under the National Parks and Endangered Species Act of 1982 to declare the Wilds a habitat for indigenous endangered animals. Theoretically, that would force Ohio's General Assembly to reinstate the Wilds' funding."

"Uh, Dad?" said Salt.

His dad covered his eyes and sighed. "I know, I know. Every single animal we've got on the place is from another continent. The only indigenous animal we're feeding right now is the beaver that dammed up the feeder stream on Mays Fork and figured out how to open the lid on the zebras' grain barrel. And as your mom keeps pointing out, he's strictly an off-line expense." His dad sighed again. "The whole point of the Wilds is to provide free-range acreage to exotics. Reticulated giraffes. Bactrian camels. Przewalski's wild horses. Flying dragons."

Salt nodded. "So have you mentioned to Mom this trip to Washington might be a long shot?"

"Your mom's kind of upset right now. The smart thing for me to do here is follow her out to Washington with a couple of changes of clothes. In case we're there for a week. Or two."

Salt's dad packed his Lincoln Memorial necktie and his one and only suit coat. "I can't believe how big those dragonlings got in a week," he said.

"Rascal doubled in weight," said Salt. He picked at the yarn ties on the bedspread. "Queenie's still the longest, but Sunshine's had two wing molts already. You should see 'em squirm out of the wheyr when they pick up the vibrations of my bike tires going up the hill. Two tons of dragon crawling around and chewing on my boots like a pack of puppy dogs. They pulled every single eyelet off my work boots and broke my watch trying to rub all the gold off the wristband. They hiss at Ham, still."

Salt stood up and took some photos out of his back pocket. "Oh, the dragon pictures came back. I sent a set to Dr. Zhao."

Actually, he had sent the pictures as part of a huge package—half scientific treatise, half fan letter. Salt wrote that it was an honor to be involved in dragon research. He wrote that he hoped the observations they were making in Ohio would further the scientific understanding of flying dragons everywhere. He wrote that he had studied every article Dr. Zhao had ever published. How soon did Dr. Zhao think he could make it to Ohio? Just roughly.

Salt had sealed the package—then opened it again. Sort of casually, like it really didn't matter, he added a couple of his best drawings of dragon snouts along with a formal India-ink portrait of Rusty snoozing among the rocks. He grabbed a pen and scrawled along the bottom of the page: "Portrait of Rusty. From your number one fan, John Salt," and slipped it toward the bottom of the stack where a busy dragonologist might easily miss it.

Salt flushed a little, thinking about it. He should have been more calm and collected. More coolly scientific and stuff. Too late now.

"Aw," said Salt's dad. "This one of Trigger and Pal pouncing on Queenie is a terrific stop-action shot. You've done a great job on the growth charts. Really great. Sure you don't mind keeping up the field observations?"

"I love it," said Salt.

"And how are things working out with Mary Athena?"

"Um," said Salt.

The truth was, Aunt Mary Athena was pretty weird. All she ever did was phone Paris for more research stuff and disappear into the garage lab for hours on end. The garage was so full of FedEx boxes and cases of imported mineral water that Salt couldn't park his bike there anymore.

But supper was the worst. On the nights it was Salt's

turn to cook, they ate regular food: tacos, macaroni and cheese, spaghetti. On her nights they ate food Salt had never heard of: shiitake, arugula, organic rampion— what kind of pretend food was that? The portions were pitiful, not that his aunt ate anything anyway. She just swallowed handful after handful of weird plant extracts and washed them all down with the mineral water she drank by the bottle. She was as skinny as ever, but Salt had put on a couple of pounds due to all the midnight raids on the fridge he'd been making because of the inadequate suppers.

"Yeah. Spud's a great old gal, isn't she?" his dad said proudly. "A real sweetheart. When I mentioned that Uncle Dinsmore would get a big kick out of seeing her again, she just got the sweetest smile on her face and said, 'Really? Well, I'd certainly love to give Uncle Dinsmore a kick.'"

"Um," said Salt again. Aunt Mary Athena's sweet smile sure looked more like a sneer to him. His dad thought his sister was wonderful. But Salt just plain wondered.

Because that funny little feeling he'd felt the first time he laid eyes on his aunt was growing. Sometimes over candlelight and couscous, her eyes would narrow into slits as she quizzed him gently but thoroughly about the dragons. Their routines, their habits, and where *was* the wheyr, exactly? And as he talked, she stared at him, the same way Mr. Eggebean had stared at him after he had opened the science room window and released his fruit flies into the wild instead of chloroforming them like he was supposed to. A stare that couldn't believe what a weenie he was. A stare that made him nervous.

So he never said anything too definite about the wheyr's location. Which was stupid. The wheyr was no secret. If she ever mentioned her interest in the wheyr during one of her infrequent trips into town, she'd find out the location in a minute. He just hoped she'd continue to stay all wrapped up in her garage lab, too busy to drive into town and quiz the locals.

His dad smiled at him. "Hey, I know exactly what you're thinking. You're thinking Spud's great, but you wish life would get back to normal, huh?"

"Um," said Salt, wondering if it was just *his* dad, or was it dads in general who lost touch with reality every once in a while.

"Look, in a week or two we'll know where we are with everything. But I just got to be with your mom. I mean, what if she decides to pick a fight at the Supreme Court level?"

Salt shuddered.

"Precisely," said his dad. "Supreme Court justices are way too old for a free-for-all."

They lugged the suitcases out the back door—"Atta girl, Loretta, how's the pretty girl," said his dad—to the car. Salt stood in the shade by the barbed-wire fence and fed Doug, the ostrich, a handful of cracked wheat and raisins.

"I'm leaving you with kind of a load," said his dad, sighing. "The dragons, school, your aunt."

"No problem, Dad. Don't worry about me, okay?"

The garage door opened. Doug raised his head, alert. Aunt Mary Athena stepped over the threshold, speaking rapid-fire French into her cell phone. She cut off the moment she spied Salt's dad by the Jeep. She gave the door behind her a quick kick with her foot. It slammed shut behind her.

"Why, Peter dear, off so soon?" she called. At the sound of her voice, Doug hooted once in alarm and bolted. Salt stared after him, puzzled. Doug was the tamest, friendliest animal on the place. He loved everybody. What could have spooked him like that?

"Yup," said his dad. "My plane leaves at six."

Aunt Mary Athena glided toward the Jeep. His dad's voice softened as a goofy look came over his face. "You're a great gal, Spud, pitching in like this." She flinched, but his dad didn't seem to notice. "This whole funding fiasco really put a crimp in your family vacation, huh? Yet here you are, not a word of complaint. I really admire that."

His aunt smiled. "Don't be silly, Peter. I'm perfectly content to enjoy the quiet charms of Spratt. John and I are having tons of fun." She smoothed her perfectly groomed hair and stroked her throat with the backs of her fingers. Her twinkly smile held the faintest of sneers. Salt checked to see if his dad caught it, but he was too busy grinning at her, so pleased and proud to have such a swell sister.

"Okay. So—I'm out of here," said his dad. "Mind your aunt, John." He frowned. "Wait a minute. You don't have a math test coming up, do you?"

"Monday."

"Hoo boy. Promise me you'll study. *Promise.*"

Salt grimaced.

"I just don't get how you can plot growth charts, compile statistics on an entire range of animals, calculate vaccine dosages in your *head*, for goodness' sake, and then turn around and almost flunk seventh grade math," Salt's dad grumbled as he got behind the wheel. "And cut the grass!" he yelled as he backed the Jeep down the driveway. "Like today!"

Salt waved good-bye. "Sure, Dad," he murmured. "Sure, sure, sure." The Jeep's taillights disappeared around the curve.

His aunt's smile disappeared. "High time he left," Salt thought he heard her say as she turned on her heel and glided across the yard. "And now for some *serious* work."

She pulled at the doors. They didn't budge. The garage had barn-style doors that swung outward into the yard, but the warm, wet winter had turned into a warm, wet spring, and the left-hand door had warped shut. She yanked on the doors again, then turned and narrowed her eyes at Salt like it was all his fault. She tapped her foot, waiting. Salt walked over, that funny feeling making his heart speed up a little.

"Here, Aunt Mary Athena, let me help you. See? Sometimes you really have to yank on it, and then—oof!—it won't close exactly, for a couple of days, but—"

"Mmm," said his aunt, brushing past him into the garage. "Perhaps you could help me with this as well?"

This was a large cardboard box on the stainless steel examination table.

"Some assembly required," his aunt muttered as she examined her face in the triple mirror. "I never have this problem in Paris."

Salt looked into the box. "A Sears Craftsman twenty-inch chain saw, huh?" he said, pulling out the owner's manual and flipping through it. "Top of the line, a truly great chain saw. This should be pretty easy. All we have to do is thread the chain, tighten a couple of connecting screws, gas it up, and let it rip."

The funny feeling about his aunt went away, a little,

as Salt pored over the schematic of the chain saw's engine. Boy, there was nothing better than the inky smell of a Craftsman owner's manual. He puttered happily, degreasing a sticky bolt rod on his aunt's new chain saw while she looked on approvingly.

Salt got so wrapped up in his aunt's latest purchase that it never occurred to him to wonder why, precisely, she needed one of Sears' finest power tools.

Chapter Eight

—⁓—

An hour later Candi Clarke stood on the Salts' back porch and fussed with the tinfoil covering a huge plate of baked goods. Candi had bugged her mom all week about the healthful properties of oat grass and seaweed until her mom threw in the towel and created a brand-new treat specially for Dr. Salt: kelp 'n' karob bars. Candi crimped the tinfoil securely around the rim of the plate. Frankly, the kelp 'n' karob bars looked and smelled like something her cat Tinkerbell had coughed up. Dr. Salt was sure to love 'em.

"Okay," she murmured. "Get psyched."

She had a lot of hopes and dreams riding on this. It was going to happen. Today, Dr. Salt was going to take Candi on as her personal assistant, because a smart kid like Candi was too good to pass up. *Très bien*! *Fantastique*! Dr. Salt simply couldn't do without her, and then boy, oh boy, oh boy! This summer it would be Hello, Paris!

The thought made her jumpy with excitement.

Candi rapped on the kitchen door. "Helloooo? Anybody home?"

No answer.

"Shoot," she muttered. "I cut softball practice to come here, and Dr. Salt isn't even—" She broke off. One of the doors to Dr. Salt's garage lab was open, and the light was on inside. Candi made a beeline for the garage. Sure enough, Dr. Salt was sitting on a white lab stool next to the stainless steel examination table, surrounded by stacks and stacks of unopened FedEx boxes.

Candi inhaled deeply. Gosh. Heaven must smell exactly like this, this incredible blend of French *parfum*, *crème de la fondation*, and nail polish remover.

And Dr. Salt looked incredibly glamorous in streamlined black closed at the throat by an offset zipper of black snakeskin. No belt this time, just a rope of South Seas pearls twined casually around her neck. Black alligator boots with spike heels and wickedly good pointed toes gave Dr. Salt's outfit the perfect finishing touch. Candi glanced down at her own shoes—thick-soled wedgie-toed things that had looked so cool this morning but now were one step away from clown shoes. How embarrassing.

There was no time to go home and rethink her outfit.

Dr. Salt looked up from the topographical map spread between her hands and straight at her.

"Well, *hi*, Dr. Salt!" cried Candi. "Mom baked today so I thought I'd—"

"Oh, no thank you, dear. I never eat in the afternoon," Dr. Salt murmured, raising her eyebrow at Candi's worshipful smile. "Food might interfere with the absorption rate of my four o'clock bladderwort supplements." She popped what looked like two dead twigs into her mouth and took a delicate sip of mineral water. "Though I do admit they smell simply divine."

Candi shuddered.

Dr. Salt looked down at the map again. "If you're looking for John, he's not here."

Candi wrinkled her nose. Who cared where Salt was? Salt was around every day of the year, every year of the decade, and frankly, Salt was . . . Salt.

"Nah, I'm not looking for him," she said. "He's over at my house watching TV with Ham."

"Mmm," said Dr. Salt. She took another delicate sip. Candi got the uncomfortable feeling she was being ignored. That was bad. An assistant Dr. Salt could ignore was an assistant who wouldn't be making the trip to Paris. Hastily, Candi opened her mouth. What had they been talking about?

"Because if he's not hanging around our house, he's

out messing around with those stupid dragons. Not that you're interested in dragons, of course. Ham dragged me out there last night. They're fat, they're smelly, they're halfway through some juvenile molt that's gonna turn them into these gorgeous adults. I mean, you should have *seen* the mom, boy, in sunlight she was like a shimmering emerald. . . ." Candi looked at Dr. Salt's sleek black-on-black outfit and sighed. She had to stop talking about color around Dr. Salt. "But in the meantime, they look like gigantic pickled eggs."

Dr. Salt looked up suddenly. Candi smiled eagerly.

"Ah. How shortsighted of me," murmured Dr. Salt. "Of *course* one of the locals would know. . . . So you've seen them?" she asked. "You've been to the wheyr?"

Candi's smiled faded a little. "Um, sure," she said. "It's not very far. Most people aren't real interested in them. I mean, *I'm* not real interested in them. It's just that my stupid brother—"

"Really?" breathed Dr. Salt. "I would have thought . . ." She squeezed the map in her hands until the edges crumpled back. It was a map of the Wilds. "I suppose I'm the last person in Spratt to know the exact location of the wheyr. Poor, poor me."

"Nah. I bet lots of people don't know. Like, they could care, know what I mean?"

"Oh, how I'd like to send a picture to my Paris office.

They think Ohio is the Land of the Bland, and so on and so forth." Dr. Salt glided silently to Candi's side. "Of course, I'd like to prove them wrong. And if I sent them a picture of something truly unique, something really cutting-edge, something like . . . you, Connie, in front of the wheyr? Holding a dragon in your arms?"

Candi snorted, yearning to be Spratt's cutting edge but grossed out at the idea of having to heave-ho a smelly dragon around.

Dr. Salt scanned Candi's plum passion lipstick and matching fingernails. She cleared her throat and said, "You're such a lovely young lady. So, ah, dynamic look-ing. Please. I'd like to send my colleagues a picture. You. A dragon. Is that too much to ask?"

Candi could hardly believe her ears. Did Dr. Salt just ask for help? She did, didn't she? That made her, Candi Clarke, the personal assistant to Orléans Cosmetics' R and D director! Heads up for Paris!

"Okay, Dr. Salt!" cried Candi. "You want a dragon? You got a dragon! But first we gotta swing by the store and pick up a couple packages of hot dogs."

Twenty minutes later, in the parking lot of Gunderson's Stop & Shop, Candi pointed out the loca-tion of the wheyr on Dr. Salt's topographical map. She snuggled back into the Range Rover's leather seat, all set. Boy, oh boy, oh boy. Softball practice would be breaking up right about now. Wouldn't it be great if Allison Fishbinder and the rest of the infield got a load of who was cruising around town behind custom-tinted windows?

Candi leaned toward the window, ready to wave. Unfortunately, Dr. Salt hit the gas, tore through the parking lot past the store's Dumpster, and swerved into an empty field bounded by a windbreak of trees and the Wilds' barbed-wire fence. "Did I mention? I'm keeping a low profile these days."

Dr. Salt drove like a wild woman. She barely kept her eyes on the road—um, grass. The Rover drove through the electronic gate at the Asian pasture. They roared past a couple of bantengs, popped a wheelie at the Père David's deer, and bounced onto the South African veldt.

They drove south along the barbed-wire fence, the one that separated the Wilds from unreclaimed coal lands. Candi looked out her window. Black, balding mountains of rock and dirt bulldozed out of the mine loomed on either side of an old gravel-bed access road that snaked through a bunch of rusted-out sheds and metal scaffolding. Disconnected power lines thicker than her arm sagged from utility poles on either side of the surface mine road.

Candi wrinkled her nose. Surface mine, that had to

be a whaddayacallit, an oxymoorthing. The strip mine went two hundred feet straight down, surrounded by eroding spoil piles of dirt and rock dotted with thistle plants whose seeds had been blown to this barren place by the wind. Funny how even scraggy old weeds exhibited the classic biological characteristics of growth, adaptation, and change, especially when one considered the—

Candi shook herself. Whoa, careful. Careful to not get all wrapped up in that thinking stuff. She was trying to quit, remember?

The Rover jerked to a stop. Candi got out. She glanced at the jagged black mountains on her right, then turned toward the green and gentle hills on her left. The contrast was amazing. It was really peaceful and clean out here now that the Wilds had moved in. Nice—if you liked the quiet, boring life. Personally, she was ready for a whole bunch of growth, adaptation, and change. Preferably in Paris.

Dr. Salt stepped out of the Rover and frowned at the size of the hill they had to climb. "They didn't do it this way when I was a girl," she grumbled as they hiked toward the wheyr. "When I was a little girl, we had high walls, sinkholes, acid ponds. Ravines piled with old truck tires. Back then, we knew exactly where to stand. *Off* reclaimed coal land. Period."

They stopped in front of the perfectly round, perfectly deep, perfectly quiet hole tunneled halfway up the side of the hill.

"Oh my," panted Dr. Salt. "I haven't walked this much in years." She fanned her face and neck with both manicured hands. "Whew!"

Candi leaned into the mouth of the wheyr and waggled a hot dog. "Here boy, here boy, here boy. Hey! Don't you hiss at me! You hiss at me, you can forget about the hot dog!"

"Bingo," murmured Dr. Salt as the first dragon—ten feet long, four hundred pounds, easy—slithered into the afternoon light. She dropped to her knees and stroked the dragon's molting scales with trembling fingers. A big old strip of dead skin came off in her hands.

Candi wrinkled her nose. Double-dee-sgusting. "That's Blackie," she said. "Or maybe Pal, I dunno. Salt has these names for 'em, but they just look like stupid snakes to me. Okay, with ten-foot wings, but still."

She eyed the last dragon wiggling out of the tunnel. Candi crouched into her windup and threw. "Strike," she called out happily as the hot dog sailed past the double row of fangs and down the dragon's throat. She wiped her fingers on the back end of her purple miniskirt.

"I'm the starting pitcher for our ball team," she said

modestly. "We were state runner-ups last year." She looked out of the corner of her eye, hoping Dr. Salt would be totally impressed, but she was wrapped up in patting that stupid dragon and hadn't seen Candi nail the pitch.

"Finally," murmured Dr. Salt. "After months of tedious research, my project is finally—" She broke off and eyed Candi.

"Let's take your picture over here with this perfect specimen," said Dr. Salt. She bustled around, herding Candi and the dragon down the hill to the Rover. It took almost every single hot dog to get that stupid dragon to curl at Candi's feet.

Dr. Salt rooted around in a toolbox in the backseat of her Rover and pulled out a cheap disposable camera. Candi tossed back her hair, threw out her chest, and pouted her lips for the camera.

"Wait a moment. I want to make this photo really fun," said Dr. Salt. She tapped her chin, thinking. "Let's pull the dragon into my Rover. We'll snake it behind the steering wheel as if it were driving."

After fifteen minutes of hard shoving, Candi gave up. "It's not gonna go all the way in," she panted.

Blackie, or whoever, its head draped over the steering wheel, its body still coiled upon the ground, opened its mouth and hissed. It sounded like a snicker.

Candi shot it a dirty look.

"Mmm. Probably needs a muscle relaxant." Dr. Salt opened the toolbox wide, and Candi glimpsed the weirdest stuff: scalpels, skin clamps, bone saws, two packages of black latex gloves, and a plastic bowl. Dr. Salt fished out a prescription bottle and shook three red pills into her palm. She poked them into the last remaining hot dog. The dragon scarfed down the hot dog and, five minutes later, went as limp as a wet noodle.

"Whoa," said Candi. "Her muscles are relaxed, all right."

Dr. Salt tucked the camera underneath a bar of the Rover's ski rack. Her eyes glittered with triumph. "I did it," she breathed. "I finally did it."

"Boy, I'll say you did. Now we're never gonna get this thing into the car," grumbled Candi.

"No, you absurd child, I meant that finally I have a—" Dr. Salt looked at the stupefied dragon. "Mmm. I see what you mean."

Just then Candi got a brilliant idea. "Hey, I know! If the rental guy gave you a hydraulic car jack and a crowbar, then we're all set!"

She could hardly believe it. Things were going so, so great. She was assisting Dr. Salt all over the place, and Dr. Salt was looking at her with a great, big, twinkly smile on her face.

"Why don't you look in the trunk, then?" said Dr. Salt, handing her the keys.

Sure enough, the Rover had both. A couple of minutes later, after Candi had jacked the dragon into the Rover, she found herself in the backseat arranging coils and coils of dragon as Dr. Salt used the crowbar to wedge them over the headrests. Candi had to hand it to Dr. Salt's personal trainer. Her upper body strength was pretty amazing.

The hind end flopped into Candi's lap as Dr. Salt got behind the wheel. The Rover rocketed off.

Disgusted, Candi pushed the smelly coils away and opened the window. The dragonstink was so strong, it made tears leak from her eyes. Her mascara started to run. Candi pinched her nose shut and breathed through her mouth. Her lipstick began to dry and crack. Tiny beads of sweat popped out on her forehead, liquefying her foundation. Candi shoved harder and breathed shallowly. If she didn't get out of this backseat quick, she was gonna suffocate. And suffocation would *totally* ruin her makeup job.

Ten minutes later, at the foot of her driveway, Candi practically fell out the door, supremely glad to be out of the dragonstink. The Rover screeched off, the dragon's tail spike dangling from the open window. Dr. Salt's disposable camera popped out of the ski rack and tumbled to the road as the Rover ran the stop sign at the intersection.

"Hey!" yelled Candi at the Rover's rapidly disappearing taillights. "Dr. Salt! You never took my picture!"

Chapter Nine

—ᘏᘏ—

That evening Salt left the Clarkes' house and biked out to the wheyr for the five P.M. observation and stats. When he got there, eight dragons caterpillared every which way over the hill. Frowning, Salt counted again. Queenie, Pal, Sunshine, Sparky, Rusty, Rascal, Trigger, and Smokey. Eight. Where was Blackie?

He climbed to the top of the hill and whistled. No Blackie. The barren landscape of unreclaimed lands glowed like molten tin in the early evening sun. He climbed down and stared thoughtfully at the eight pairs of amber eyes staring back at him. Hard to tell, but the dragons seemed . . . spooked about something.

He let a Holstein out of the cow pen and walked her over to the dragon pasture. Without Blackie, the hunt was sloppy and disorganized. The cow kept trotting through the dragon-sized gap in the encirclement. The pack finally gave up the stalk and just chased the cow up and down the pasture until the poor thing keeled over from exhaustion. Then they ate her.

Salt nudged between Pal and Sparky. He scooped some cow intestine into a bucket and climbed the hill. He banged on the bucket with his clipboard and yelled Blackie's name. No sign of her.

As Salt climbed down, he noticed the tire tracks of a heavily laden sports utility vehicle churned into the mud by the barbed-wire fence. Uh-oh. One of the animal techs must have been out checking on the dragons. Mom was going to flip when she came home and saw the request for overtime.

Salt finished the routine stats, then climbed the hill again and scanned the sky. Maybe Blackie's wing structure was more developed than her nestmates'. Maybe the old girl just flew away.

The sun began to set. No sign of Blackie. Salt began to worry. Dragons were diurnal, extremely sensitive to the sun's position in the sky. It wasn't an issue of light exactly, for even the brightest of full moons, Dr. Zhao pointed out, would not persuade a pack of dragons to remain aboveground. No, once the sun went down, the pack remained strictly underground, the opalescent sheen of their scales glimmering against the dirt walls of the wheyr all night long. "Dragons seem to enjoy a night-light as much as humans do," Dr. Zhao had written.

Despite his worry, Salt had to smile. That Dr. Zhao. What a funny guy.

Salt biked home a little after dark, his thoughts all wrapped up with Blackie's disappearance and dreams of the day he'd finally meet Dr. Zhao face-to-face. Shake that great man's hand. Get his autograph, even.

Aunt Mary Athena was out, the house quiet. Salt entered his field observations into his notebook and fixed a big supper. An hour later Loretta flapped home for the night. Salt gave her an old bone and locked the aviary door.

Back inside the house, Salt spread out his homework assignments in messy piles all over the dining room table. He filled one of his mechanical pencils and opened his math book.

He stared sightlessly at the word problem on page 242. Where was Blackie? It bothered him that not all nine dragons were snuggled down for the night. Was Blackie okay? Was she safe underground somewhere, lighting up the darkness with her glistening scales? Did she miss her brothers and sisters?

Salt picked up the pencil and stared at the lead hovering over a blank sheet of paper. Okay, maybe it was a weenie thing to admit, but Salt kind of missed his mom and dad, too. Things in Washington weren't good. His dad had e-mailed yesterday. His mom had already had one very close call right outside the Senate chambers involving the junior senator from North Dakota, a reporter from the *Washington Post*, and a German tourist.

Without actually thinking about it, Salt touched the pencil to the paper. A nice, curvy line flowed across the whiteness. Snakey, like a dragon's spine.

A couple of hours later, Salt was hunched over a fresh sheet of paper, lost in his drawing, shading a series of dragonwings in the various molt stages from juvenile bud to mature wing. He was so wrapped up in getting the crosshatching just right that when his aunt's Rover peeled up the driveway and screeched to a halt outside the dining room windows, Salt jumped a mile.

He hurried to the kitchen, flicked on the porch light, and opened the back door. Loretta, her head under her wing, rattled her tail feathers, annoyed at all the human commotion when decent birds were asleep. Aunt Mary Athena, one hand on the railing, one foot on the bottom step, glanced at the aviary, disgusted.

"Awful bird," she muttered. Her gaze lifted to Salt, standing in the doorway. "Ah, yes. You. I forgot about you. You could be a problem."

She smiled at him, the sneer unmistakable. "What

shall I do with you, hmm? It's too late to check you into a really good hotel. You'll just have to stay out of my way."

Salt's heart thumped, that funny little feeling scream-ing in his ear. "I saved your supper," he stuttered. "F-f-fish sticks, nothing special."

She drifted up the porch stairs. "How thoughtful. Really quite a thoughtful little boy. However, I am tired of pussyfooting around. Pretending to be what I'm not—all twinkly smiles and fun-loving aunt. So let me spell it out for you: I don't eat fried foods. Ever." She brushed him aside as she strode through the kitchen. "I've forgotten my ten o'clock supplements," she mur-mured, "in all the excitement."

Salt followed her into the dining room and watched her glide up the stairs to the second floor. She returned in less than a minute, carrying a leather shoulder bag that chinked faintly of bottled mineral water.

"I won't be home until late," she told Salt. "And then I'm going straight to my lab. So don't wait up."

At the mention of her lab, Salt grimaced. Aunt Mary Athena had reorganized the garage until it was barely recognizable. All the counters had been cleared of the comfortable vet clutter—cotton swabs, sterile suture packs, a bunch of old taxonomy textbooks—and were packed with makeup. Rows upon rows of gold-on-white

Orléans bottles and tubes and flasks crowded the shelves, lined the counters, filled the whole room. Lipstick. Cologne. Hair goo. The smell was worse than dragonstink any day.

Aunt Mary Athena had banished the lawn mower and leaf rakes to a leaky corner of the back porch. She paid the DeFelice brothers to set up a floor-to-ceiling magnified mirror with a white leather barbershop chair bolted to the cement floor in front of it. The brothers had ripped out the overhead shop lights and wired in three rows of track lighting that lit the front of the garage like a stage but left the back half dark. Only the deep freezer and the stainless steel examination table—with the gassed-up chain saw squatting at one end—remained the same. The garage was creepy and girly, both. Salt never went in there anymore if he could help it.

"I have some extremely important research to conduct," his aunt was saying. She stopped by the dining room mirror and stared deeply at her reflection for a moment, turning her face side to side. The pile of Salt's drawings on the table behind her, also reflected in the mirror, suddenly caught her eye.

"What's this?" she asked sharply, turning away from the mirror and picking up a drawing. She thrust it toward Salt.

It was a sketch of Blackie twined around a tree. Salt

grinned at the drawing's excellent vertebra articulation, the perfect shaping of the—

"Well, did you?" snapped Aunt Mary Athena. "Draw this?"

"Yep," said Salt modestly. "It still needs work, though."

Dead silence. Salt winced to see his aunt staring at him in utter disbelief.

Maybe she didn't like it because she thought drawing dragons was dumb. Maybe she thought the perspective was weak. Maybe she thought he traced it. Salt hurried to cover up the embarrassing silence.

"Yep. Sure, sure, yep, it's my drawing, all right. I didn't trace it, if that's what you're . . ." Salt cleared his throat. "You can have it if you like." Since she had a death grip on the corner of the paper and a fierce frown on her face, it was probably a good idea to let her keep it. "Because I have plenty more where that came from."

Salt waggled his fingers and gave a fake laugh. "So. Um. Gosh, I know it's not a great French masterpiece or anything, but maybe you can take it along when you visit Uncle Dinsmore. He always likes my—"

"Uncle Dinsmore? Uncle Dinsmore is a JERK!" yelled Aunt Mary Athena, her deep voice three octaves higher with rage. "I wouldn't visit Uncle Dinsmore on a bet! I wouldn't visit Uncle Dinsmore if you paid me!"

She sure didn't sound like a twinkly aunt-on-vacation anymore. Salt backed up, stumbling over chairs, knocking into plant stands, desperate to put a little distance between himself and Aunt Mary Athena.

She thrust out her chin until her jaw cracked. "For your information," she sneered, "Uncle Dinsmore is the one who saddled me with that ridiculous childhood nickname."

Backed up against the philodendron, Salt blinked. "You mean the one Dad always calls you? Spud?"

"Don't say it!" screeched his aunt. "Don't you dare say it! Sure, I had a tiny roll of baby fat around the middle when I was twelve. But that was years ago! Years and years ago!" She flung out her toothpick arms and demanded, "Do I look like a tuber? Well? Do I?"

"Y-y-you sure don't, Aunt Mary Athena," squeaked Salt. "No tubers here."

"Precisely," she sniffed. "Don't you forget it. And I'll thank you"—she rattled Blackie's drawing at his scared-stiff face—"to keep your pencil out of my business." Her eyes narrowed into slits. "Get the picture?"

"Yes, ma'am," squeaked Salt. "Sure do."

She spun on one high heel and strode out of the room. Salt heard her high-heeled alligator boots click-clack across the linoleum, across the back porch, down the steps. Backed up against the tippy plant stand, Salt brushed a couple of philodendron leaves off his face and watched her through the dining room windows. Aunt Mary Athena tossed her shoulder bag and Blackie's drawing into the Rover. The drawing sailed to the ceiling, then fluttered gently into the back, coming to rest on top of a large, blanket-covered lump stretched out on the backseat. Cursing and muttering, his aunt got behind the wheel and slammed the door. The Rover squealed off into the night.

Salt hung around with the plants until his heart got back to seminormal. He went into the kitchen and fidgeted nervously, taking a dinner plate out of the oven and nibbling at one of the fish sticks he had saved for his aunt. The house was still. Silent. Waiting. He shoved the plate into the fridge and beat it upstairs to the safety of his room.

Salt lay down on his bed fully dressed and listened to the furnace blow hot air through the heating ducts. The curtains at his window billowed in the warm air, the motion calm and soothing. He thought about his parents. He thought about Blackie. He wondered about his aunt. Slowly, his eyes drifted shut. And Salt fell asleep.

Some time after five A.M. a distinct whine, an unpleasant hum, rattled the glass in his bedroom window. Salt rolled over and opened an eye. Only one thing made a sound like that. A chain saw. It had to be a chain saw. Running in the garage.

Salt clapped his hands over his ears. Jeez, what kind of person sawed down trees at five o'clock in the morning?

A totally creepy person, that's what kind. Visions of Aunt Mary Athena swinging a chain saw in the garage lab made him way too nervous to move. No way was he going downstairs, not to investigate, not to go to the bathroom, even. He was staying put.

A shout of triumph echoed out of the garage. The noise stopped. Salt took his hands away from his ears and listened—which was a mistake. The silence was definitely worse than the noise. The silence got so bad, it chased him out of bed. It scooted him across the hall, down the stairs, out the kitchen door. Salt eased past the lawn mower and leaf rakes, careful not to knock them over. His boots made no sound as he tiptoed through the dewy grass.

The doors to the garage were closed except for the rain-warped boards along the bottom. Cold light escaped beneath the gap. Salt crouched on his hands and knees, put his eye to the hole—and froze.

"It's Aunt Mary Athena," whispered Salt, "and—holy smokes!"

That cold, merciless light hid nothing from his horrified gaze as the chain saw again roared to life. A thin black shadow moved slowly, deliberately, across the length of the stainless steel examination table, the chain saw blade slashing, tearing, hacking.

He was going to pass out. Or puke. Or both. Blindly, Salt crawled backward away from the terror in the garage. His left boot smacked sharply into the porch steps. Salt spun around and scrambled up the stairs, through the kitchen. He grabbed his waterproof parka and tool belt from the hall closet, jammed a pair of work gloves into his pocket, and sped out the front door.

Salt thundered down the driveway, burned past Empire Steer's feedlot, and swerved around the cap rig on the natural gas well at the edge of the Wheelers' cow pasture. He slowed down at the intersection of Coal Hill Road and Route 146, gasping for breath.

A rooster crowed. The sky lightened over Spratt. Salt listened for the clickity-clack of high-heeled alligator boots or the cannon boom of a Range Rover in hot pursuit, but all was quiet. His gasps turned to wheezes. Not the ghost of a sound from the direction of his house. Thank goodness she hadn't seen him. Thank goodness he had gotten clean away. Salt turned and limped painfully into town.

He staggered through the parking lot of Gunderson's Stop&Shop before he collapsed facedown on a lone shopping cart left outside the store entrance. He lay there, completely exhausted, as the birds twittered sweetly overhead and the streetlights blinked out one by one.

This was it. He was going to stay right where he was. His left cheek was turning into a waffle from being pressed against the metal shopping cart, but that was okay. No matter how uncomfortable he got, it was still better than thinking about what he'd just witnessed in his aunt's garage lab.

His aunt . . . Blackie . . . Blackie . . . his aunt . . .

He just wouldn't think about it, that's all. Salt lay limply across the shopping cart and willed his thoughts into a mindless blank. TV-watching blank. The remote in one hand, a box of cheese crackers in the other.

Blackie . . . his aunt . . . his aunt . . . Blackie . . .

His ear, pressed against the shopping cart, began to itch. Salt scratched. He sneezed. His nose began to drip. He mopped it with his sleeve. Then he shifted his weight around a little, trying to get comfortable. His coat twisted and bunched into his armpits. His left foot went to sleep. He stamped it awake. Salt twitched and rubbed and scratched and sniffed for a few more minutes as he thought about it nonstop. *Blackie. His aunt.*

Salt sighed. Who was he trying to kid? Going limp wasn't going to solve anything. He was the sole eye-witness to a bloody and unnatural crime. Aunt Mary Athena had broken at least ten federal laws governing the use of animals in research. Every second he delayed

108

in calling the cops was giving her a chance to break ten more. Was that what he wanted?

Salt groaned and straightened up. Slowly, he untangled his chilly fingers from the cart. Slowly, slowly, he rubbed the corrugated marks from his cheek. It was time to face facts.

"Aunt Mary Athena's gone off the deep end," he told the shopping cart.

He walked over to the phone booth outside the entrance to the Stop & Shop. Boy. She was gonna kill him when she found out that her own nephew was the stool pigeon. After he called the police, he'd have to join the Witness Protection Program and disappear. They'd let him write a farewell letter to his parents, probably. Then they'd give him a nose job and a pair of fake glasses and send him to live at an orphanage in Idaho.

After that lonesome thought, Salt had to stand around for a couple minutes and breathe deep. It was tough, but he finally got enough courage to pick up the receiver and dial. His finger hovered in the air over the phone's push buttons.

Then he remembered the big sign taped to the door of Spratt's police station: "Closed until April third. Gone fishing with Mickey!" Officer Al, Spratt's one-and-only policeman, was off on a two-week vacation to Disney World.

"Good grief," muttered Salt. "Now what?"

He tried to think. Basically, it was impossible to find anybody with an interest in the dragons on the weekend. The attitude of most people in Spratt was that as long as the dragons didn't poop in their yards or mess with the chickens, they'd just ignore 'em. And the vet barns were deserted. Once the Wilds' animal techs heard his parents were gone, they'd all taken off for a costume party thrown by the Biology Department at Ohio University in Zanesville. His parents were still in Washington. Hmm.

Salt picked up the phone. He dialed the operator and asked her to look up the number of his parents' favorite bed and breakfast in Washington, D.C.

"That number is two-oh-two, five-five-five, nine-four-two-seven," said the operator.

Salt dug around in his tool belt and came up with a pencil stub. "Okay. I need to make that a collect call."

"I'm connecting that number," said the operator.

"Uh, could you repeat that? I didn't get a chance to—"

The operator had already cut out. The phone rang and rang. After about ten rings, somebody finally answered.

"Capitol Bed and Breakfast," yawned a voice.

"Will you accept a collect call from—" began the operator.

"You got me outta bed on a Saturday for a collect call?" snarled the voice. "Get yourself a real job, lady!" The phone slammed.

"Operator, wait!" cried Salt desperately. "I didn't get the number written down!" Too late. She had bumped him to a recorded message. "Your call cannot be completed as dialed. Please hang up and dial again."

Sadly, Salt stuck the pencil stub back in his tool belt. He dug around in his pocket and came up with three quarters, two nickels, and a hoof-pick. He stared at the loose change for a moment, then flipped through the Spratt phone book chained to the side of the phone.

He found the number for St. Mark's rectory. Father Aloysius was six months from retirement and hard of hearing, but a priest's whole life was one of community service, right? He'd be bound to help. Full of optimism, Salt dropped his first quarter into the phone and dialed.

"Father Aloysius! This is John Salt! I have a big problem with the dragons!" he yelled into the phone.

"Dragging, hey?" barked the priest. "In my day drag racing was a *sin*, same as dancing."

"No, Father, I said 'dragons'! Drag-ONS! The kind that—"

"You hooligans ought be sitting up straight and paying attention on Sunday morning instead of slouching there and smirking about what went on Saturday night!"

"But I—"

"Furthermore, it is six-thirty in the morning and I am an old man!" The phone slammed.

Salt sighed. He used the second quarter to call the meanest, toughest human being in all of Spratt. Salt shuddered at the thought of calling and talking, but he had to do it. Aunt Mary Athena wouldn't stand a chance against the school's vice-principal. The phone rang twice.

"What?" bellowed a man's bass voice.

"Uh. Hi, Mr. Park. Is Ms. Park there? This is John Salt, one of her seventh-grade students."

"Good grief, kid, it's going on seven o'clock on a Saturday morning! She's been hitting the garage sales for a good forty-five minutes already. Next time call around six, why doncha?" The phone slammed.

Salt looked down at his last quarter. It was a complete weenie thing to admit, but he was feeling lost. Confused. Scared, even. He desperately needed a friend.

Allison Fishbinder's cool face drifted into his thoughts. So maybe this was the excuse he'd been looking for to call Allison. They could team up and really use this adventure as a deeply personal bonding experience. The more Salt thought about it, the better it sounded—until he remembered their last conversation. "It's not your *hands*, Salt. It's your *hair*. It's your *shirt*. It's your

112

shoes. You're gonna stink up the whole *day*. Yuck."

Salt winced.

Okay, so the dragons needed more than just a beautiful face. They needed somebody brave. They needed somebody resourceful. They needed a hero. Somebody like . . . well, like Dr. Zhao, for instance. Boy, Dr. Zhao wouldn't stand around and dither, wondering who to call, listening to his stomach growl. He'd be too busy hiking out to the wheyr, ready to protect the dragons with every fiber of his being, even if he had to throw his own body between them and some creepy, chain saw–wielding makeup lady. Who just happened to be his aunt.

Salt winced again.

Well, he wasn't a hero like Dr. Zhao. Not even close. A guy who spent most of his free time slouched in front of the TV watching nature videos and snacking right out of the box wasn't a guy who would throw his body in front of a chain saw.

Salt thought about it some more. He dropped his last quarter into the phone and called the Clarkes'. The phone rang and rang. Ham picked it up, finally.

"Listen, Ham," said Salt. "I'm swearing you to secrecy. I need your help. Meet me behind Gunderson's store as soon as you can."

Salt looked up and noticed the sale posters in the

window. Two-percent milk. Seedless grapes. All-beef hot dogs, eight to a pack. Three packs for a dollar.

"Whoa," murmured Salt. "Wait a minute. I got this idea. We'll need ten dollars, about. And Ham? Did your mom bake yesterday? Because I am starving."

Chapter Ten

—⁓—

Zit soap, foundation, blush, eyeliner. Candi yawned. Good thing today was Saturday. Powder, mascara, eye shadow, lipstick. Today she could stand in front of the bathroom mirror and use it all.

Candi yawned again. The first light of morning glinted on the dinged-up nickel faucets in the Clarke family bathroom. Almost seven o'clock. Crazy, getting up this early. Saturday was stupid chore day, so the earlier you got up, the more chores you had to do. Well, forget that. Her plan was to sneak out of the house without doing *any* chores. Which was why she'd been up for a whole half hour already, dressed in skinny black jeans, Ham's good white Sunday shirt under a black vest, and boots.

Regretfully, she touched the vest. Good-bye, purple miniskirt. *Au revoir*, pink rhinestone hair clips. Now that she was Dr. Salt's assistant, she was going to have to dress the part. Like she was on the way to a funeral . . . or France. Candi grinned happily as she pinned a dish towel around her neck and leaned into the mirror.

"Okay," she said to her reflection, "get psyched. Me, on her doorstep first thing. Perfect makeup, perfect hair, perfect clothes. Me, the perfect assistant. Me. In Paris. Got it?"

She hummed as she bent closer to the mirror. Boy, oh boy, oh boy. She could just see herself dressed in black, pale makeup, heavy on the mascara, looking all high-fashioned and serious on a rain-soaked street in front of the Eiffel Tower.

And this time she got to visualize the scene for a whole minute before her traitor mind went to work on it—before the black cashmere turtleneck morphed into a lemon yellow tie-dyed T-shirt. Candi sighed. She tried hard not to like it, but who can resist lemon yellow tie-dye? She let the shirt stay. Big mistake. Next thing the sky turned azure, the trees blinked in orange, crimson, umber—the Eiffel Tower turned bronze and gilt in the mellow autumn light. Before Candi could get a grip, her visualization had run amok in fabulous, full-color Paris. Drinking icky mineral water and lime under an outdoor café umbrella shining so blue in the sun it made you want to scream with joy. Strolling through castles jammed with tippy red velvet chairs and gold leaf ceilings and acres of white marble floors. Crossing old stone bridges covered in dusty emerald ivy and silver moss. A sleek black poodle on a rhinestone leash prancing down the Champs Elysées. And what about that famous art museum with the glass pyramid out front? Bet that was *loaded* with pictures of people in terrific clothes from the seventeenth century and—

Candi heard Ham's bedroom door squeak open. His feet shuffled across the hallway toward the bathroom. Boy. She could just picture him. Head down—eyes closed—scratching his stomach underneath his White Sox shirt—stumbling to the toilet.

A huge, reverberating thump bounced off the bathroom door. The key jiggled in the lock.

"Ow! My head!" cried Ham.

"I'm in the bathroom!" yelled Candi.

"Well, get out! I gotta go."

"Just a minute."

Ham waited about five seconds before he pounded on the door.

"I SAID just a minute!"

"For cryin' out loud, will you kids knock it off?" yelled their dad from the bedroom.

"If you're up, there's hazelnut coffee cake in the

breadbox," called their mom from the bedroom. Downstairs, the phone rang.

"C'mon, Candi!"

"What is your problem, Ham, you can't wait a minute!"

The phone rang and rang.

"For cryin' out loud, somebody get the phone!"

Ham shuffled off downstairs. Candi waited a second, then opened the bathroom door and dashed to the top of the stairs where she could hear better.

"Hey, Salt. Nah, not really awake, and Birdbrain is hogging the bathroom so I can't . . . yeah. Yeah? Yeah. Okay. See you." Ham hung up.

Candi beat it back into the bathroom, totally disgusted with her brother. What kind of conversation was that? Not a thing worth eavesdropping on.

Five seconds later Ham was pounding on the bathroom door. "I *still* gotta go!"

"And you *still* gotta wait!"

"If you kids don't stop screaming out there, I am going to duct tape your mouths shut!"

"There's a batch of deeply Dutch chocolate muffins if you'd rather eat those," called their mom. "Look in the aluminum pan next to the toaster oven."

"You let me in right now," growled Ham.

Candi opened the door and breezed by. "Hurry it up.

I got a lot more to do in there."

By the time Candi got her makeup applied, her parents had gone back to sleep and Ham had gone, period. He had left a big old mess in the kitchen. Judging from the mountain of rich, moist coffee cake crumbs and balled-up pieces of plastic wrap all over the counter, Ham had taken the rest of the coffee cake along for Salt.

Candi put her hands on her hips and pouted. After her dad had taken one bite of the kelp 'n' karob bars, he made her mom promise to go back to baking with sugar. So now what was she supposed to do? Knock on Dr. Salt's door empty-handed? Some assistant. Assistants glided around noiselessly in the background and handed the boss stuff just when the boss needed it: paper clips, reports, schedules, coffee . . . coffee cake. Jeez. If only Dr. Salt were the kind of woman who cheated on her eating plan occasionally. But it was impossible to imagine cool, disciplined Dr. Salt with a dot of melted butterscotch on her chin.

Heyyy. What about flowers? The Wheelers' cow pasture was full of those weedy things Mrs. Wheeler was forever twisting around old dead grapevines and selling to Kountry Kupboard Kollectables for a ton of money. Some of those weedy things, maybe, and a couple of daffodils swiped from the clump by the front porch, wrapped in tissue paper left over from Christmas. She saw herself on Dr. Salt's front porch, holding out a dew-bedecked bouquet of lovely spring flowers to a surprised and grateful Dr. Salt.

Perfect.

Out in the muddy field dotted with piles of cow flop, her jeans soaked, her arms scratched, her sinuses full of pollen, Candi bent over and yanked at one last stupid weedy thing. The stem, full of sap, refused to break. She gnawed at it until it broke off, and spat out a few bitter green stem strings.

"This," said Candi grimly, "had better be worth it."

Half an hour later, Candi stomped through the crumby kitchen and shoved her sparkling, dew-bedecked bouquet into the fridge. She stomped upstairs to take a shower, change her grimy black-and-white outfit for a clean black-and-white outfit, work over her makeup, and brush her teeth.

By that time her parents were up. Her dad spotted her sneaking out the back door. Next thing Candi knew, she was stuck cleaning out the garage. She had to pretend to shove boxes around all morning until her dad finally, finally! got into the car and drove off to the lumberyard. The second he backed down the driveway, Candi ducked back into the house, hurried across the kitchen, grabbed her bouquet from the fridge, and scrammed.

So it was nowhere near first thing in the morning when Candi and her flowers arrived at the Salts' back door. It was almost eleven o'clock, and nobody was home.

"Shoot," muttered Candi. "And Dr. Salt's from the city. I bet she locked the door." She rattled the knob. Sure enough.

Candi looked down at the sparkling, dew-bedecked flowers. The weedy things had oozed sticky yellow sap all over her fingers. The daffodils had attracted a large, persistent bumblebee. Candi waved away the bee. She had to put those stupid flowers down. Like right now.

Fortunately, somebody had left the kitchen window open to the glorious spring morning. Candi climbed through the window, stepped over the pile of dishes in the sink, and started to look through the kitchen cupboards for a vase. She opened every single cupboard—which wasn't strictly necessary since she had found a row of dusty vases behind the second door she opened, but hey, how could she know those were the only choices unless she looked around a little? And after having snooped her way through the kitchen, dining room, and study, Candi found herself outside, making a casual beeline for the only place she was really interested in anyway: Dr. Salt's garage lab. Candi yanked on the door until it swung open.

"Ooo, I knew it! She's got it totally set up," she

breathed. "A replica of her Orléans research lab pictured in *Makeup from the Edge*! It's so clinical! So researchy! And it's full of *makeup*!"

Funny. In the end she was drawn not to the rainbow rows of blushers and lipsticks, but to the stainless steel table, upon which sat a large kitchen bowl full of blackish-bluish sludge. The sludge glittered in the glare of the overhead spotlights. It bubbled: slow, languid bubbles, like a thick stew set to simmer on the back of the stove. Candi touched the rim of the bowl. The plastic felt hot and soft, melting a little from hours of heat.

"Don't touch that," commanded Dr. Salt from the opened doors behind her. She strode into the garage and, with oven mitts, removed the bowl and set it on a low shelf. As she turned around, Candi got a good look at her face.

There was something weird about it. True, Dr. Salt didn't have an ounce of makeup on, but that was only part of the weirdness. Candi stared and stared until she finally got it. Dr. Salt's wrinkles were gone. Her skin stretched smooth and firm around her eyes, across her forehead. The two deep frown lines that had dug in like train tracks at the corners of her mouth were completely erased.

Candi blinked in astonishment. Dr. Salt's face looked peeled and pared and—with that green tinge to her complexion—perfectly parboiled. Accessorized with a sprig of parsley, a pat of butter, and those terrific pearls, Dr. Salt could go as Madame Potatohead for Halloween.

"What are you doing here?" demanded Dr. Salt.

She seem distracted, rushed. A faint but very definite sneer kicked at both corners of her mouth as she gazed at Candi through narrowed eyes. Candi wondered at the heavy attitude change, but hey, a good assistant would stay calm and upbeat, overlooking her boss's occasional snit fits.

"Well *hi*, Dr. Salt! Don't you look, um, well rested! Ya see the flowers I brought? I was gonna bring over some duckweed coffee cake or something, only Mom went back to sugar. Anyway. So I'm all set to assist you again today, Dr. Salt, in any way, shape, form, size, content—"

"Cookie—"

"Candi."

"Why did your mother name her children after food? I believe it indicates a mild psychological problem." With an impatient frown, Dr. Salt removed her oven mitts. Candi double-crossed her fingers, curled her toes, and prayed that Dr. Salt's next words would be "Get me a bottle of mineral water and the latest fax from Paris, willya?"

"How do I get rid of you, hmm? If I give you a makeover, will you go away?"

Candi gasped. "You'd . . . you'd do a makeover? On me? A makeover featuring Orléans products? Done by the head of Research and Development? On me?"

"You have to promise to go home afterward."

"You *got* it, Dr. Salt!"

In a flash Candi had her face scrubbed clean. She fell into the white leather chair next to the *bleu/vert* palette shelves. Dr. Salt drew on one of the unmistakable Orléans white smocks with the world-famous MO insignia embroidered over the pocket. She fanned out a row of jars, bottles, and tubes with the practiced hand of a poker player who cheated.

"Take a journey with me," murmured Dr. Salt, totally transformed into a soft-spoken, deferential skin technician, "to the mountains of Lucerne in the Swiss valley, where Marie Orléans—naturalist, herbalist, and world-class entrepreneur—first combined Swiss mountainside botanicals containing one-hundred-percent natural hydraserum inflatables and other totally meaningless mumbo jumbo into *this*." Dr. Salt held up a shapely green glass bottle.

"Orléans alfalfa emulsifier," breathed Candi.

"And this?"

"Blue-stem restructuring gel."

"And this?"

"Ooooo palettes shadeaux des yeux in chartreuse,

verdigris, and *puce!"*

Dr. Salt simpered, the skin of her face stretching and bouncing like a rubber mask. Her fingers pinched Candi's cheek, assessing the moisture content of her skin. "How well you know the Orléans' line, *mademoiselle."*

"Boy, oh boy, oh boy. My face in Orléans cosmetics! Ya know, this year in math I did an independent study project where I made a bar graph comparing the cost per pound of various cosmetics—"

"Tilt your head *à gauche.* Mmm. I see you pluck your own eyebrows."

"—and Marie Orléans' line costs way, way more than anybody else's! Ow!"

"We'll do a little eyebrow reshaping—"

"Ow!"

"—and start with *le cleanseur."*

"Hey! I cost-analyzed this very cleanseur! See, once you take it out of this eensty-weensty bottle, weigh the lotion, figure out how many bottles of lotion make up a pound, and multiply that number by the cost per unit, Orléans Tout Fait Cleanseur costs six hundred dollars a pound! Isn't that amazing?"

"Next, the Fondation du Mozambique."

"Two hundred fifty dollars a pound!"

"With just a dab of under-eye concealer."

"Whoa! Awesome! That's the priciest item of the line,

coming in at one thousand, nine hundred, sixty-seven dollars and eighty-nine cents! Per pound! Go heavy, okay?"

"Cheek couleur, mascara, lip liner, and filler—"

"Three hundred fifty, nine hundred eighty-seven, a hundred forty-three dollars, and the filler's like five hundred something," whispered Candi breathlessly. Her cheeks and lips felt stiff and heavy.

"Loose matte powder to prevent smudges, *et voilà!*" Dr. Salt whipped off her smock and turned Candi's chair so that she faced the mirror. Dr. Salt stood behind the chair and said smugly, *"Regardez, mademoiselle!"*

"Hmm," said Candi. She stared at her magnified reflection in the mirror and wondered for the first time if Dr. Salt was maybe not all she was cracked up to be.

It took an effort to turn her head this way and that in front of the mirror—the thick layer of foundation felt like it was about to crack into a hundred pieces. The blush on her cheeks extended all the way into the hairline at her temples. Dr. Salt had penciled in a new, much darker set of eyebrows that topped her forehead like two scrawny caterpillars. And the color blend was all over the palette: mint green next to amber next to deep scarlet red. Candi stood up and took a step back from the magnifying mirror. Her face snapped into focus.

Well, she sure didn't look as she yearned to look: like

an extremely smart, extremely pretty research assistant on her way to Paris. Her makeover was miles away from smart. And it was miles away from pretty. Frankly, she looked, she looked . . .

"Like a runway model," murmured Candi. "A really beat-up, chain-smoking one." Allison would totally love it. Candi winced.

"Exactly," cooed Dr. Salt, leaning past Candi and gazing deeply into the mirror. "Isn't this how every young girl longs to look?"

"Um," said Candi. She fell back into the white chair and swiveled this way and that in front of the mirror, trying to admire her face, the face of glamor. Okay. It was ugly and garish. But it was ugly and garish done with top-of-the-line Marie Orléans cosmetics, applied by the experienced hand of Dr. Salt herself. Candi shook off her disloyal thoughts and said: "Boy, oh boy, oh boy. I am looking at a hundred and fifty bucks' worth of makeover, easy."

Dr. Salt gave Candi a once-over in the mirror. "You look sweet, darling. Quite *à la mode*." Dr. Salt's gaze left Candi's makeover and traveled back to her own face. "Pleasant, being a lowly colorist again."

She leaned forward and stroked her smooth green throat. "Though I much prefer being the head of Research and Development. And after a lot of years of hard work and personal sacrifice, that is precisely what I am."

Dr Salt's gaze wandered past the mirror to something high up on a shelf slightly to the left and behind Candi's head. "Lots and lots of personal sacrifice," she murmured. "Not many R and D directors would leave the nightlife of Paris for a place like Spratt, just to conduct a little field research in antiaging, for instance."

Candi tuned out Dr. Salt and her boring talk about wrinkle cremes. She swiveled all the way around and stopped short. What was the deal with the crummy spotlights in here? Dr. Salt looked positively . . . reptilian.

"But this wrinkle creme is worth it. Look at my skin. Not a wrinkle, nor jowl, nor sag. Not a bag to be seen. My brilliant, groundbreaking research has managed to turn back the hands of time!"

"Yeah, but your skin's turning green, Dr. Salt. Kinda blackish green, actually. Not a great look."

Candi stopped, unsure. Could green be the hot new trend in skin tones for fall? True, weird cosmetics fads popped up every season, but . . . *green skin*?

Frankly, green was not a skin tone she could picture herself actively promoting. On the other hand, she was Dr. Salt's assistant now. A loyal part of the Green Skin Team. Candi caught another glimpse of her funhouse face in the mirror. She felt her happiness dim a little.

Boy. Being Dr. Salt's assistant was not all French *parfum* and trips to Paris. Things were getting complicated. She was starting to get a funny little feeling.

"Mmmmm," said Dr. Salt, once again staring past Candi's head to a high corner shelf. "The formula needs tweaking, I admit. The dragonic serum needs to be diluted. But with what? Perhaps a few extra-strength plant toxins . . ." Dr. Salt drifted past the garage doors murmuring, "Leave any time within the next five minutes, Constance."

"Candi," muttered Candi, astonished. "My name is Candi." Was losing a couple of wrinkles so gosh-darned important to Dr. Salt that she didn't care if her skin turned green?

Puzzled, Candi spun around and looked up and slightly to the left, up to the thing that had drawn Dr. Salt's gaze, up to the high shelf in the corner. A dragon's head, severed at the fourth vertebra, had been propped up between a travel guide to the Swiss Alps and a gallon of astringent. It was so dead, it looked real.

Chapter Eleven

When Ham finally turned up at the Stop&Shop, Salt grabbed a cart and headed for the meat aisle.

"So which ones are on sale?" asked Ham.

"These," said Salt. "Eight to a pack. Perfect."

Mrs. Gunderson adjusted her bifocals and blinked in amazement at the mountain of hot dogs Salt and Ham unloaded at her checkout. She looked at Ham's backpack. "You boys going on a camping trip?"

"Well. More like a long hike and a picnic," said Salt semitruthfully. He frowned. "Is there sales tax on food?"

Mrs. Gunderson shook her head. "How many packages you got there?"

"Thirty-six," said Ham. He took the plastic-wrapped hazelnut coffee cake out of his backpack and started cramming in package after package of hot dogs. "We're definitely gonna need a bag, Mrs. Gunderson."

As they passed the phone booth just outside the store entrance, Salt stopped to dither.

"It's going on eight o'clock. Jeez, we've wasted a couple of hours already. Maybe I should try my parents again. Or maybe we should go to your house and call."

"My parents catch me, I'll be stuck cleaning the bathroom and doing laundry for the rest of the day," warned Ham.

"Aunt Mary Athena could be at the wheyr already . . . with her chain saw." Salt shuddered and hiked the grocery bag firmly between his arms. "We better get going."

Salt and Ham ate most of the coffee cake as they cut through the parking lot, past the Dumpster, and onto the Asian pasture. A herd of Persian onagers, the world's fastest horselike species, snorted and stamped at the strange smells of sugary coffee cake and sweaty boy. The onagers chased them down a hill and past the cattail marshes of a reclaimed pond. The miniature stampede set off a pair of nesting egrets. The honking, stamping, flapping, braying frenzy made Salt and Ham stick their fingers in their ears as they hightailed it toward the peaceful South African veldt.

They walked along a faint pair of tire tracks, the grass flattened, maybe, by a heavily loaded sports vehicle. As they turned onto the dirt track heading south along the barbed-wire fence that separated the Wilds from

131

unreclaimed territory, Ham looked over his shoulder, then left and right.

"Okay," said Ham. "The coast is clear. Nobody's following us. So what's up with your aunt?"

Salt closed his eyes, remembering. He was on his hands and knees again, peering through the gap at the bottom of the garage doors. A tall figure stood in the shadows on the far side of the stainless steel examination table. Slowly, slowly, the figure set down a chain saw, peeled off a pair of black latex gloves, and leisurely examined its manicure for chips.

Salt's eyes popped open. "My aunt's gone off the deep end," he said. "Last night I heard a noise in the garage, so I got up and . . . and . . ."

On the steel table under those pale, busy hands lay a scaly body faintly touched with green and gold, its tail disappearing into shadowy coils on the floor.

"And she had Blackie s-s-stretched out on the table," whispered Salt.

His horrified gaze had flown along the dragon's spinal column, searching for three trapezoidal markings transverse across the fourth vertebra. Trouble was, there had been no fourth vertebra.

Ham gulped. "You mean?"

Salt nodded.

There had been no fourth vertebra, because there

had been no head. A few drops of blackish-bluish blood fell from the chain saw's toothed blade onto the cold concrete floor, where they hissed and bubbled. His aunt muttered something nasty and swooped to put a small plastic bowl under the chain saw drips. Her bronze hair gleamed under the lights. And she had laughed in triumph.

"Aunt Mary Athena murdered Blackie," Salt whispered hoarsely. "But why? What in the world does my aunt want with a dead dragon?"

"We shoulda known your aunt was wacko," said Ham. "Coach always says you are what you eat, and she ate pretty weird."

"What's to stop her from killing another dragon?" said Salt. "Or all of them? The dragons are in terrible danger. We gotta hide them, like right now. And we only have until dark to move them."

"Well, where are we gonna find a big enough hole to hide ni—I mean, eight—dragons? Don't tell me we're digging one, because it's not too late for me to go home and start washing socks," said Ham.

"No, no, I've got a plan. My aunt's been away from Spratt for thirty years, right? She doesn't remember much about the terrain. So we take the dragons cross-country and hide them in one of the underground mines. They're what—five miles west of the boundary fence of the Wilds, maybe? I'm pretty sure the dragons can locomote that far. We get 'em settled down for the night, then you and me hike back to town and call my folks."

Salt felt his arms growing numb at the pull of the heavy bag. His heart sank at the thought of a ten-mile round-trip hike. Ten *miles*, good grief. And another three miles back into town and a phone. He hoped *he* could locomote that far. "Boy, I wish I knew what my aunt was up to, exactly. What she did next with those chain saw drips sure doesn't make any sense."

The dragons, lazily sunning themselves in front of the wheyr, snapped to attention the second they smelled Salt.

"Sorry, guys, it's not Holstein time," he apologized. Salt dropped the heavy bag of hot dogs on a small rock ledge jutting out of the hill next to the wheyr, and rubbed his aching shoulders. "We got something else going on today."

He stopped, listening. The distant sound of a foreign-made motor revving hard and fast came echoing out of the hills of Asia.

"Bet that's your aunt, Salt," said Ham, "Driving out to claim her next victim."

Sure enough, Salt glimpsed a flash of cherry red between the hills. The next moment he saw the Rover screech to a halt and beep impatiently at the herd of onagers grazing across the dirt road. The onagers reared up and charged. More angry beeping.

"She knows," squeaked Salt. "She knows I saw her in the garage last night." Salt had a short, terrible picture of doom—his aunt looming over his poor sawn-off body, a growling chain saw in her hand.

The Rover eased through the milling onagers and turned onto the dirt track that led to the wheyr. The car bumped to a halt at the foot of the hill.

Aunt Mary Athena got out. She stared up at them for a long moment, shading her face beneath both manicured hands, then reached into the Rover and pulled out a large black hat with a deep, shadowy brim.

Salt shivered.

Queenie reared up beside Ham. Her tongue flicked briefly in the direction of Aunt Mary Athena. Ten seconds later, the dragons had vanished down the wyrmhole. Who could blame them? Salt yearned to dive for the dirt and belly crawl right after them.

His aunt stopped ten feet below the wheyr. "So. Here you are, John," came her voice from beneath the hat. "Taking care of my"—she inhaled quickly—"the—dragons." The hat brim turned from side to side. "Where are they?"

"Where are who?" Salt's voice squeaked hideously.

He cleared his throat and tried again. "Where are who?" he boomed.

Aunt Mary Athena tapped one alligator boot impatiently. "The dragons, the dragons," she snapped. "No need to yell at me, John. I have excellent hearing."

"Well, uh, hmm. The dragons? Uh, yeah, the dragons." Salt scanned the horizon. He had always been terrible at lying, which was too bad because now he was stuck with the truth. "They must be around here somewhere," he said lamely.

Ham kicked Salt's shin. "The truth is, ma'am, they're hiding down their wyrmhole."

Aunt Mary Athena folded her arms. "Oh? And why would the dragons presume to hide on such a sunny day, hmm?"

"They don't care much for baseball," said Ham. "The dragons, I mean. Last week Russ Nelson smacked a line drive out to right center and beaned old Trigger right on the—"

"You're playing baseball . . . out here?" asked Aunt Mary Athena.

Salt rubbed his nose, hiding his grin. True, he personally couldn't lie for spit, but Ham was another matter.

"Yep. See, we usually practice at the school, of course, but the girls' team will head up to state again this year, no question. Sure, my sister is a birdbrain, but she's a pretty good pitcher. The boys' team ain't so hot—fact is, we were at the bottom of the league last year, and now that the season's started, I can't say we've improved a whole lot—so us guys graciously agreed to let the girls practice at the school's ball diamond. That means we come out here and use the field right down there. 'Bout the right size and it's level more or less, so we just throw down a couple of car mats for bases and play our game."

"John plays on the baseball team." Aunt Mary Athena's voice sounded flat and extremely suspicious.

"Oh yes, ma'am. Best second baseman we ever had," said Ham earnestly. "We won three games last year on the strength of Salt's defensive skills. He is pure magic with an infielder's glove."

Salt blushed beet red, even though he went nowhere near an infielder's glove if he could help it. Ham sure sounded convincing. John Salt, hero at second base. It had a nice ring to it. And Aunt Mary Athena certainly seemed to be buying it.

"Mmmmmm," she said thoughtfully. "If there is going to be a whole crowd of witnesses—I mean, *people*—coming—"

"Let's see. There'll be the guys, of course. The coaches, the equipment manager. A whole bunch of parents will set up lawn chairs and hang around and bash the coaching. So that'll be, what? Twenty, thirty people."

"Wait a minute. What's this grocery bag full of hot dogs for?" said Aunt Mary Athena sharply.

Salt dug his fingernails deep into his palm. It was his fault. What a dope—to leave all those packages of hot dogs right out in plain view. His aunt could hardly miss them.

"We're gonna have a weenie roast," blurted Salt. "After practice." Ham gave him an approving nod. "Hope somebody brings some buns, because we totally forgot."

There was a long silence. Salt held his breath.

"Well," said his aunt, annoyed. "I was hoping for a little peace and quiet while I examined the dragons more closely. No special reason, of course. Just . . . curious. They're really quite fabulous animals, are they not?"

"Fabulous," agreed Ham.

"Quite," echoed Salt.

Aunt Mary Athena tugged at her hat. "I'll be sure to come out later this afternoon after everyone is gone." Salt saw the flash of a smug and greedy smile beneath the brim. She turned and walked away.

"Yeah, and so long to you, too, Dr. Salt," yelled Ham. Silently, they watched her climb into the Range Rover and zoom off. "Whoa. Did you see her sneer at us?"

"We have *got* to get the dragons out of here before she comes back," said Salt grimly. He dug a package of hot dogs out of the grocery bag. "C'mon."

Easier said than done. The dragons had been spooked by his aunt's unexpected appearance. They refused to crawl out of the wheyr. Salt stuck his head down the wyrmhole and sweet-talked until the dragons finally burst out of it, knocking Salt and Ham flat on their butts. They scattered like rabbits through the tall grass.

It took more than an hour and six packages of hot dogs to find them, calm them, and coax them into some form of marching order, but eventually the last dragon squeezed under the barbed-wire fence that separated the Wilds from the barren landscape of unreclaimed coal lands. Salt and Ham kicked around some dirt and grass to disguise the belly trails under the fence, and off they caterpillared, south and a little west.

Three hours later Salt dropped to his knees and fell over on his back in a puff of grit. Ham flopped down next to him.

"I gotta head back, Salt," Ham said. "I got a ball game in Sarahsville at four and I gotta pack, because I'm staying the night at my grandma's."

Salt squinted at the sky. "It's after one o'clock. Slow going on this stuff." He kicked at the coal rubble beneath his boots. "Slower than I thought. But we're about halfway to the underground mine system." Salt pulled an EPA land use map out of the pocket on his tool belt and consulted it. "The Number Three entrance is the closest. We should make it before sunset."

"How many hot dogs you got left?" asked Ham.

"Fourteen packs. And the dragons don't look a bit tired."

True enough. The dragons looked ready for another three-hour slither. Most of them stretched out upon ground, fanning their fully opened wings. Sunshine reared back and raised her wings above her head. *Clap. Clap, clap, clap.* A huge whoosh of air blew back the hair on Salt's head. Like a yawn that goes around a classroom, the other dragons reared back to clap and shake their wings. Salt counted the beats as the wind whistled in his ears. The dragons had begun the wing-clapping behavior almost from the moment Salt and Ham had led them past the Wilds' barbed-wire fence.

"Honest, Salt, I got to go," repeated Ham. "I'm the only decent ballplayer they got." And he left.

Alone with his thoughts, Salt shivered. *His aunt . . . Blackie . . . Blackie . . . his aunt.* Poor old Blackie. What a way to go.

Oh, it wasn't so much that Blackie was dead. Salt had observed a hundred different food webs operating in a hundred different biosystems, and frankly it was a miracle that none of the dragons had bought it from genetic malformation, or disease, or even from their unfortunate habit of sunbathing on the warm asphalt of Route 146. One of these days a coal truck was going to take the curve too fast and *whamo*—dragon roadkill. The bad thing was not that a dragon had died, because that's what happens. Birth. Life. Death. No, the bad thing was that Aunt Mary Athena had killed in the name of Science. And if she killed once, she'd have no problem killing again. And again and again.

Frowning, Salt jotted down a few wing-clapping observations in the margins of his map. Then he drew a quick sketch of Sparky as he tried to figure out the best route to Number Three, a tiny forgotten speck in the far southwest corner of these fifty thousand acres of unreclaimed land. Salt repeated that comforting number. Fifty thousand. Fifty thousand.

A wilderness big enough to get lost in. Where Aunt Mary Athena'd never find them. Especially here. The coal lands he and the dragons had trekked onto might have been stripped out just last week. A blasted moonscape of rock and crater and hill stretched as far as he could see. Not a blade of grass or dandelion seed blown by the wind had established itself in these bleak hills of debris. The same warm spring breeze that had ruffled his jacket and played gently upon the green grasses back at the Wilds smelled cold and dead out here. Yep. Cold and dead.

Cold like a cold-blooded makeup researcher. And dead like a dragon.

Salt nibbled meditatively at one end of a hot dog as he tried to puzzle it out. Okay. So Aunt Mary Athena hadn't just dropped in for a nice family visit. She had heard about the dragons and decided to check them out. But why? The only things Aunt Mary Athena ever talked about were the fabulous Paris parties and wrinkle creams. In fact, she always got a distracted look in her eye whenever he talked about the dragons. Like she was thinking about something really profound, something his tiny little mind could never grasp.

He shook his head. Give it up. He'd never figure out his aunt, never. So he tried it from the dragon end of the equation.

Dr. Zhao's letter was crammed full of hard scientific data about dragon physiognomy and behavior, but none of that seemed to be any help right now. In fact, Salt had a funny feeling that what had happened to Blackie had left the rational, scientific world of dragonology far behind. His thoughts drifted to the bowl of gently bubbling dragonblood he had glimpsed from his hiding place behind the garage doors last night. How carefully she had collected every drop. It had to be something about dragonblood. Definitely something.

"Well. There's all those ancient myths and legends," murmured Salt doubtfully. At the sound of his voice, Trigger undulated over and laid his head in Salt's lap.

"Your blood's supposed to make me understand the language of birds," he said, scratching Trigger behind his ear folds. "It can heal a Chinese hero of his wounds. But not a regular Chinese guy, huh? Drink it and it gives you visions of the future. Pour it on your shoes, your shoes'll sprout dragonwings so you can fly around delivering messages from the ancestors."

Salt stared off into the middle distance. "But why would you want to do what Aunt Mary Athena did? Smear it all over your face, I mean. Let me tell you, last night in the garage, Aunt Mary Athena looked sicko."

He dropped the nibbled hot dog into Trigger's open mouth. "All I know is we better not hang around until I figure out what's up with my aunt. I bet she's in her Rover right this minute, looking around for us. She may not know about the undergrounds, but she's not dumb. Once she figures we've left the Wilds, she'll scout out the countryside. And we better not get caught aboveground."

He shoved Trigger off his lap, stood up, and winced. Boy, his feet hurt. "C'mon, guys. This way."

Chapter Twelve

When Candi got home from Salt's house, she carried the phone upstairs into her bedroom. She closed the door and stared at the phone. She stared at the phone because if she stared at the phone, she could avoid staring into the dresser mirror and seeing her weird hundred-fifty-dollar reflection. And if she could avoid her reflection, she could avoid the uncomfortable thought that went with it: The hand that had smoothed the foundation was also the hand that had sliced off a dragon's head.

Candi winced. Who was she trying to kid? She couldn't *stop* thinking about it. But Dr. Salt really wouldn't do something like that—would she? Maybe Dr. Salt was just driving around minding her own business when the dragon in her backseat suddenly attacked, and Dr. Salt was forced to defend herself. Or maybe the dragon just got sick and died. See? There could be some perfectly logical, innocent explanation.

On the other hand, that dragon hadn't looked vicious or sick, either one. And Dr. Salt had seemed triumphant at having a drugged-up dragon curled in her Rover and at her mercy. Face it. Dr. Salt did the evil deed. And Candi—who had done all the initial jacking up and wedging in—had made it possible.

Candi winced some more. Boy, oh boy, oh boy. All she wanted to do was work side by side with her personal hero and finagle a trip to Paris. Now it was beginning to look like she had been the unwitting accomplice in a dragon murder. Life was so unfair.

Candi picked up the phone and dialed. Maybe the second-most-popular girl in Spratt shouldn't admit it, but she was lost. Confused. Scared, even. Boy, oh boy, oh boy, she needed a friend. Somebody who cared. Somebody who took her seriously. Somebody like Allison Fishbinder.

The minute she heard Allison's voice, though, Candi realized that she couldn't just blurt out what was on her mind. Dragons were definitely a weenie topic for Allison. It'd be better to make a little small talk, first. Sort of ease the conversation around. And she had better sound all cute and perky about it too.

"Allison, you will never ever guess who just gave me

a free Orléans makeover!" she squealed tiredly into the receiver.

"That is so cooooool!" cried Allison, after Candi had explained again who Dr. Salt was, exactly. "It sounds like a hundred-and-fifty-buck makeover, easy."

"That's exactly what I thought," said Candi, sighing.

"Gosh, I bet you look just like a runway model."

Candi slowly raised her eyes, glanced in the mirror—and winced. "Yeah," she said sadly, "I really do."

"Ooo, I am sooo jealous!" said Allison. "Listen, I am coming right over."

Uh-oh. The last thing she needed right now was Allison Fishbinder coming over. Allison was sure to take one look at Dr. Salt's makeover and fall head over heels in love. She'd insist that Candi make *her* over—and once the most popular girl at Spratt Grammar showed up wearing the chain-smoking-model look, everyone would want it—which meant that Candi would be doomed to wear this ugly makeup for the rest of the school year.

It gave her a headache just thinking about it. Well, she just had to fix her face before Allison got a look at it. That was all there was to it.

"Um, Allison, this isn't such a great time," began Candi. Fortunately, her dad came home, just then, slamming the kitchen door and bellowing up the stairs.

"For crying out loud, Candi, you call that garage *clean*? What did you do, shove a couple of boxes around and call it quits?"

"I'm on the phone, Dad!" Candi bellowed back.

"Well, hang up and get back to work!"

Candi turned back to the phone. "Listen, I gotta go."

"Well, how 'bout later?" Allison cleared her throat. "Will Ham be around, you think?"

"Yeah, sure," said Candi absently, wondering how anyone, even an evil R and D scientist, could ever think that puce lipstick was going to catch on as a hot spring color. Just the name *puce*. Ew. "See ya."

Candi dragged herself out to the garage and spent the next hour shoving boxes around. She went inside, washed her hands, and slowly ate a cheese sandwich over the kitchen sink, careful not to smudge her puce-lined lips. She dragged herself out to the garage and looked around.

"Good enough," she said.

Every box had been shoved around at least once. The leaf rakes and snow shovels were piled semineatly in the far corner. Her dad's workbench was thoroughly dusted. The only thing left was the floor.

Candi got out the push broom and looked at it distastefully. Sweeping, ugh.

She checked her watch. A little after two o'clock.

Plenty of time for a break.

The broom handle clattered onto the cement floor as Candi beat it into the house. She snuck up the stairs into the bathroom, pulled out every single cosmetic she owned, and shook her head mournfully. Pitiful, just pitiful. What in the world was she supposed to accomplish with this bunch of junk?

Candi stood in the bathroom and yearned. Her heart yearned for all the beautiful Orléans colors and textures just a short bike ride away in the Salts' garage. But even as her heart yearned hotly, her brain clicked coolly, thinking, thinking, thinking. Always thinking, worse luck.

For starters, Dr. Salt's research was totally screwy. There were serious problems with her methodology. Where were the test tubes full of pigments? The charts and graphs showing experimentation with new color mixes? The books on color theory? The latest issue of *Makeup from the Edge*? The only thing Candi had seen in the lab that could even remotely be considered an ongoing experiment was that bowl full of blackish-bluish sludge Dr. Salt had been so touchy about.

"And wrinkle-free, green skin," she murmured aloud. "Hmm."

Ham came home. He thumped upstairs and pounded on the bathroom door. "Jeez, Birdbrain! Get out of the bathroom for once!"

"I'll be out in a minute!"

Candi arranged her face into her I've-got-a-toad-for-a-brother grimace and flung open the door. Ham brushed past, covered with coal dust, knees bleeding, smelling worse than a dragon.

"You look real ugly with all that makeup on," he said.

"Well, you oughta know ugly. You're lookin' at it every morning in the mirror. Where have *you* been?"

"With Salt and the dragons at the wheyr." He rummaged around in the medicine cabinet. "You seen my toothbrush?"

Candi crossed her arms and rolled her eyes. Ham was such a dope. "What in the world did you do? Crawl down in the hole and eat lunch with 'em?"

"Sorta. I'm taking the toothpaste. The only thing Grandma has is that old lady baking soda stuff."

Candi got quiet. Real, real quiet. She studied her fingernails. They needed a buff. "So did you notice anything different about—"

Ham looked at her sharply. "About what?"

Candi opened her eyes real wide and innocent. "Hey, just a question, I don't know—what made me ask? Let me think . . . so, um, *did* you notice anything different about the dragons?"

"Uh-huh," said Ham. "But Salt swore me to secrecy."

He stomped out, leaving the door swinging open.

Candi turned back to the mirror, disgusted. "So does Salt know his aunt killed a dragon or doesn't he?" she muttered. She propped her elbows on the counter, rubbed her eyelashes, and stared at the mascara clumps covering her fingertips.

The phone rang. "I got it!" she yelled as she galloped into her room. It was Allison, probably, seeing if the coast was clear, garage-wise. Well, Candi would just have to put Allison off again until she could think of a way to fix her face.

Big surprise. It wasn't Allison. It was Salt's dad.

"Hi, Candi. Is John there, by any chance?"

"Sorry, Mr. Salt. Ham was home a minute ago, and he said Salt—um, *John*—was at the wheyr."

"Darn. I've been trying to call home all afternoon, but somebody left the fax machine on and Mary Athena must have turned off her cell phone. Listen, Candi, could I ask you for a huge favor? Would you go over there and tell John and his aunt that we'll be home first thing on the morning of the thirty-first? We're bringing a VIP houseguest along with us, so this part is very important—tell John to please, *please* mow the lawn."

"Gotcha, Mr. Salt. Morning of the thirty-first, houseguest, please mow. No problem. I was sorta on my way over there anyway."

"Helping my sister out while we're gone? That's great. You're a lucky girl. Spud's one in a million. Give her a hug and tell her we'll see her soon. Thanks, Candi."

Candi hung up the phone, totally energized. Now she had the perfect reason to drop by Salt's house. True, she wasn't about to give dragon-slaying Dr. Salt a hug—Candi shuddered—but hey, maybe Dr. Salt wouldn't be home. Then Candi could slap a note on the back door, and the garage lab would be all hers. All she needed was access to the full line of Orléans cosmetics, half an hour, and she could fix her train wreck of a makeover.

She could go home, Allison could come over, and they could linger over every single, wonderful makeover detail. Candi smiled gleefully.

But when she got to the Salts' house, the garage doors were wide open to the late afternoon sun. Dr. Salt was standing behind the big steel table smoothing moisturizer into the cracked and scaly skin on the backs of her hands. Beside the bottle of moisturizer was a plate covered with tinfoil.

Shoot.

"Ah, Colleen," said Dr. Salt without looking up. "Have you come to be my little assistant?"

"I guess," said Candi reluctantly.

She stared at the black-clad figure of Dr. Salt, wishing with all her heart that she could just go back to where she was that morning and simply follow wherever the great woman led. But Candi had done a whole bunch of thinking over the last couple of hours. And she had to admit it was really starting to bug her, this funny feeling about Dr. Salt's mysterious makeup research. Something big. Something important.

Something terribly wrong.

"Your brother called," Candi said, taking a steadying breath and daring to look up on the shelf where the dragon's head rested.

The head was gone. Candi blinked, puzzled. Had she dreamed the whole thing? She stared at Dr. Salt, at the small, wicked smile that played around the corners of her mouth as her pale, busy hands rubbed, and rubbed, and rubbed.

Candi shivered.

"Oho, my brother?" repeated Dr. Salt in a flatly amused, cynical voice. "And what is the earthshaking message from Peter?"

And another thing: Dr. Salt treated her like a dimwitted child who had to have everything explained in words of one syllable. Like everything Candi said was a big dumb joke, even if all she was doing was relaying a simple phone message, for crying out loud. Boy, oh boy, oh boy. Talk about rude.

"He said he'll be home next week on the thirty-first."

Dr. Salt put the cap back on the moisturizer bottle with stiff fingers. She opened a drawer next to the sink and rummaged around. "Mmm. I have to tell you, everything is going excellently. My field research is complete, my formula well on its way to success. I even got to putter around in the makeup again, thanks to my dear little assistant Sandy."

"Candi," said Candi. "For the last time, Dr. Salt. My name is Candi."

"Is that not what I said?" Dr. Salt took out a prescription bottle full of little red pills, the same pills she had used to dope up that dragon Blackie, or whoever. She closed the drawer and lifted the tinfoil from the plate.

Candi blinked, astonished. A mountain of HoHo's, Ding Dongs, and Twinkies covered the plate. Candi tried to imagine Dr. Salt in the snack aisle at the Stop&Shop, popping pond scum pills and reaching for the coconut cupcakes. Good grief.

Candi tore her gaze away from the plate. Now was not the time to get distracted. She had to stay focused. "So. The thirty-first. That's next week Friday."

"Mmm. Too bad I won't be here to say good-bye. My plane leaves tomorrow night." Dr. Salt waggled the plate full of junk food. "I am looking for my nephew, John Salt. I need his . . . help."

Dr. Salt straightened up. In the mellow afternoon

light from the open garage doors, Dr. Salt's smooth, hairless green skin glowed with health. But the woman's fabulous hair was falling out. Clumps of brittle Etruscan bronze drifted past her shoulders and caught on the rope of pearls.

Candi wrinkled her nose. Dr. Salt sure could use a deep cleansing facial and a hot oil hair treatment. And a change of clothes. Wearing the same outfit two days in a row was totally gross.

But what was really strange was her sudden interest in her nephew. "Salt? What in the world is Salt good for?" asked Candi.

Dr. Salt raised a green eyelid. "I went to the wheyr this morning, fully intent upon collecting a fresh specimen. Naturally, I was disappointed to meet John and his little friend there. Still, the delay has turned out to be to my advantage. I retreated to my lab and, in the silence, I began to think. All afternoon I pondered my original hypothesis in the light of the unfortunate side effects I've been experiencing. And I designed one final experiment."

Dr. Salt frowned distractedly at a Twinkie, totally absorbed in thought. "Fool that I was," she murmured. "Of *course* it was not a superficial change to the upper dermatological layers. It was an alteration to the very molecular structure of the skin cells. Basic protein strands fused with the dragonic—" Dr. Salt broke off and glanced at Candi. Her blue eyes glittered with desperation and triumph.

"No matter. The point is, I need to correct a small error in my original computations, and to do that I need a substantial amount of John's . . . help."

She checked her watch. "Baseball practice ought to be breaking up. I believe I'll drive out to the wheyr and offer my dear nephew a ride home. He'll be tired after all that second baseman business, ready for a little light snacking. And besides, John and I are Salts. Blood relatives. And blood relatives ought to share . . . experiences whenever possible, don't you agree?"

Candi was speechless. Salt—at second base? Was Dr. Salt insane? Salt didn't know the difference between an infielder's glove and home plate. Candi's funny feeling grew.

Dr. Salt picked up the plate of snacks and brushed past Candi. "*Au revoir*, you absurd child."

Dr. Salt was leaving. Candi's eyes widened. Forget about Salt, about her funny feeling. Here was a heaven-sent opportunity to fix her face. "Hey, Dr. Salt, do you mind if I—" She pointed to the makeup mirror and rows of cosmetics.

"Help yourself," Dr. Salt said. "Just don't be here when I get back."

155

"No problem. Half hour, max," said Candi eagerly, her suspicions about Dr. Salt's bogus research totally forgotten. This was her chance! Boy, oh boy, oh boy. Candi turned to the shelf of cleanseurs as the Rover drove off.

Twenty minutes later, though, the Rover squealed into the driveway, almost crashing into the garage. Candi jumped—and smeared *écrivan Victor Hugo* lip liner all over her chin.

Shoot. Her second Orléans makeover ruined. And it had been perfect.

"Empty," bellowed Dr. Salt. She slammed the plate of Twinkies onto the table. "The wheyr is empty. My twerpy nephew and the rest of my specimens have run off." She stamped one alligator boot, then strode over to the mirror and looked, turning her face this way and that. "I don't have time for this. John had no right to run off like that. I am so angry, I could just . . . kill that boy."

"Sure. Like you did to Blackie or whoever," Candi muttered, rubbing grumpily at her lip-lined chin. It came to her suddenly that she didn't like Dr. Salt very much. Envied her, sure. Go to Paris with, absolutely. But follow her blindly wherever she led?

Dr. Salt whirled around. "I heard that! I have excellent hearing and I heard that!" Poised in front of the mirror with her hands on her hips and her thin, black body outlined by cold track lighting, her blunt, curving nose casting shadows over her receding chin, Dr. Salt was a monstrous snake rising out of the mirrored glass. "Perhaps I've been nursing a viper at my bosom. A treacherous little assistant, hmm? I thought you were on my side."

Candi could not believe her ears. "You're calling me a snake? Me?"

"You told him, didn't you? Didn't you? You told John all my research secrets!"

"Oh, sure, like I even *know* any of your research secrets! You never confided in me, never said *squat,* so I had to like totally *figure out* what you're cooking up in—"

"You're FIRED!" bellowed Dr. Salt.

That did it. Candi was really steamed.

"Forget it, Dr. Salt! You can't fire me because I quit!"

"That's the problem with entry-level employees," hissed Dr. Salt. "No loyalty, no discretion—"

"Who'd want to go to Paris with a green-skinned, skinny, old—"

"Old?!"

"—bossy *old* dragon lady anyway!"

Dr. Salt pulled off the tinfoil and grabbed the bottle of red tranquilizers at the edge of the plate. "Well! After I get this tiny problem in the formula worked out, my antiager wrinkle remover smoother exfoliate face creme enhanced with dragonblood will make me the toast of the Paris cosmetics show."

Dr. Salt shook her fist until the pills rattled. She threw the tranquilizers into her toolbox, grabbed a land compass from the instrument table, and stuffed a topographical map of the Wilds into her coat pocket.

"You might have noticed, Connie, that I am extremely goal oriented concerning this face creme. And I am close. So close. I will let nothing stop me. Do you hear? Absolutely. Nothing." Dr. Salt grabbed the toolbox, stomped out of the garage, got into the Rover, and roared off.

"You don't have to get so cranky about it," called Candi sulkily. "I got goals too, ya know." One of which—getting to Paris, France, in time for the Institut des Beaux Visages Vendors Show in June—was just not working out.

Candi frowned. She took a piece of gum out of her back pocket and unwrapped it. Well, she was in too deep, had gone too far to back off now. She had to figure out what Dr. Salt was up to. Why she was out at the wheyr so much, what the sudden interest in her nephew meant. So, even if it was a total weenie thing to do, she was gonna do it. Candi was gonna think about stuff. On purpose.

She stuck the piece of gum in her mouth and started

chewing. What had Dr. Salt said? Stuff like her twerpy nephew was a specimen. Basic protein strands fused with dragonic . . . and that thing about an alteration to the very molecular structure of the skin cells.

Candi chewed faster.

Well, it was obvious what Dr. Salt had been talking about. Basic protein strands, simple. Deoxyribonucleic acid. Good old DNA.

One thing was clear. She was totally grateful to Mr. Eggebean and his back issues of *Science and Nature*. The magazine had done a great three-part article on the latest developments of the Human Genome Project. And Candi had read every word.

Chapter Thirteen

—ᴍ—

Salt slumped against a boulder, sweating, filthy, coughing up coal dust. All afternoon he had avoided the old mine access road just in case his aunt decided to climb into her Rover and check out unreclaimed territory. But going cross-country had been tough. The dragons had struggled up every slag hill, sinking underbelly-deep into the loose, shifting debris. Every slither had kicked up a choking cloud of grit.

Salt coughed some more, then wiped his mouth and nose on the sleeve of his parka. He watched the dragons, strung out in a line and very tired now, creep slowly over the hill and down to the gritty road. Salt glanced at the sky. An hour until sunset. Underground or not, once the sun set, the dragons would refuse to travel. The old Number Three was still half a mile away. They'd never make it going over the hills. Their only chance was to follow the road.

Queenie reached him first. She hissed and gripped his forearm between her fangs in a gentle, reproving bite.

"It's not far now," he reassured her. He patted her bony snout. "We'll risk the road. The road will be lots easier. Real firm so you won't sink in and—"

Then he heard it. As the dragons humped over the loose scree and onto the road, he heard it, the sound he had been dreading all day. Faintly over the hills, from far, far away came the contented purr of a finely tuned British engine.

"Holy smokes!" gasped Salt. "It's my aunt!"

Aunt Mary Athena was driving onto unreclaimed land. That was bad enough—but what if she'd gotten hold of a map? She'd realized what an underground mine would mean to a pack of dragons on the lam. And once she figured out the whole mine system was serviced by the same road, what was to stop her from driving down and examining the mineheads one by one? Number Six. Number Fourteen. Number Five . . . Number Three. Salt shivered.

Desperately, he looked around. This was the planet's worst place to hide eight tired dragons and one nervous twelve-year-old. The spoil piles crowded in close, towering over the road. Even if the dragons could make the climb back over the hills fast enough, their belly trails would be clearly outlined by the late afternoon sun. Aunt Mary Athena couldn't possibly miss them. So that was useless. Their only hope was to stay down on the road and head for the Number Three as fast as they could. Once he got the dragons underground, he'd think of something. He hoped.

Salt broke open the last package of hot dogs. The fresh, enticing smell of hot dog drifted past his nose. Drool filled his mouth. Desire for a hot dog gripped him. He had had nothing to eat all day but half of Mrs. Clarke's hazelnut coffee cake, and those couple of bites from the end of Trigger's hot dog—but that had been hours ago. His poor body was starved for protein. Salt clenched the hot dogs possessively to his chest.

Just a lick. Just a lick, just a nibble, just a bite. His stomach gurgled. This whole thing was such a nightmare anyway, surely he deserved another hot dog, just one more measly hot dog, and anyway maybe he could just sort of let his aunt catch up with the dragons—the whole thing was so hopeless anyway—then he could go home and eat and take a shower and watch a little TV and put up his poor, tired feet on the coffee table and fall dreamlessly asleep and the next morning would be filled with sunshine and quiet and birdsong. . . .

Salt swallowed painfully. Queenie regarded him, her snout cocked questioningly to the side. Her tongue flickered in and out, smelling the air full of hot dog. She waited patiently for him to extend his hand and offer it to her, her reptilian eyes filled with an ancient sadness.

"You think I'm going to run off and leave you here, don't you?" Salt murmured. "Bug out on the snakes." He squatted and looked straight into her amber eyes. "Well, I'm not. I just had a weak moment. I'll probably have a couple more, but I'm not giving up." He straightened and listened uneasily to the engine purring in the north. "At least, I don't think I am."

He tried to smile but couldn't. "You're the greatest thing that ever happened to me," he whispered. "I can't let something bad happen to you guys."

Salt tightened his belt. He threw Queenie the hot dog and set his face southward. "C'mon guys. We gotta scram."

Salt tossed hot dogs to Pal, Sunshine, Sparky, Rusty, Rascal, Trigger, and Smokey as they slithered down the road behind him. He whistled encouragingly, clapped his hands briskly, but always, even over the *scritch-scratch* of belly scales sliding over the roadbed, he could hear the Rover's engine throb.

They followed the road past a sharp curve. A rusty gate set between two iron posts barred the road. The gate was shut to its post with a single loop of an old metal coat hanger. Salt could just make out the lettering on a tin sign bolted to the gate:

WARNING

UNDERGROUND MINE AREA

PROCEED WITH EXTREME CAUTION

WEIGHT LIMITS STRICTLY ENFORCED

"See?" said Salt. He unhooked the coat hanger. "We're almost there. Just keep yourselves spread out a little. We don't want the roadbed to fall through into one of the mine tunnels."

The undergrounds had been reclaimed long ago. Brush and brambles gave way to scrub pines and black locust trees. The dragons perked up as the trees got bigger and closer together, the trunks draped in poison ivy and grapevines as thick as Salt's wrist. The smell of moss and mold and honeysuckle lingered in the air. An owl hooted. Salt's hopes rose. They were gonna make it. They had to.

"C'mon, guys," he urged. "This way."

The sun began to set. A long ray of evening light touched some bushes across the road—and suddenly, two orange eyes blinked straight at Salt.

He froze in terror. The seconds ticked by. The eyes stared. Trembling, Salt turned on his flashlight and shone

164

it into the bushes, ready to cut and run if he had to.

"Whoa," he murmured.

A set of iron rails, furry with reddish orange rust, glittered in the flashlight's beam. The tracks had been cut off and bent into circles at the edge of the road. In the setting sun, the dead stops looked just like tiger's eyes. Embarrassed but relieved, Salt walked over and peered down the track.

"Whoa," he murmured again.

He was looking down an old mule track into Number Three. A hundred and fifty years ago, miners had dug out coal with pickaxes and shovels. Mule teams pulled out the loaded coal cars, which ran along narrow gauge railway track. Mules hadn't been down this way for a hundred years. Salt looked around. Neither had anyone else. And for the first time, the sound of his aunt's Rover made Salt grin. Let her drive around all she wanted. The dragons were about to disappear into a hundred and fifty years ago. Become the stuff of myth and legend.

"Perfect," he mumured.

Salt herded the dragons down the mule track. The dragons balked at the acid smell of rust, the harsh scrape of pitted iron against their bellies. The rock walls on either side of the track scaled higher and closed over their heads. The last of the sunset narrowed to a thin red band above the canyonlike walls. The dragons' traveling sounds echoed down the track. Sunshine and Trigger clacked their jaws, relieved to be almost underground again. Rusty's folded wings rubbed gently against the rock walls. They passed an old wooden pipe still trickling a thin, brown stream of wastewater. Pal lapped at the mossy spout, his tongue scratching like sandpaper.

The mule track curved gently to the left, then ended suddenly in a wall of total darkness. Salt clicked on his flashlight.

"Sealed. Of course it's sealed," Salt muttered in dismay, shining his light over the double-barred oak door spiked into the rock. "I'm an idiot." He yanked at the rusty iron chain looped through a padlock as large as his head. The chain barely rattled.

Old smells of swollen wood and wet dynamite made him sneeze. The sneeze made him cough. Salt choked on his own spit as a car zoomed down the road overhead. A couple of seconds went by. Brakes screeched.

"I am a double idiot," Salt wheezed.

Why hadn't he bothered to drag some underbrush in front of the mule track? The old iron rails had been scraped free of rust and rubbed shiny by the dragons' underbellies. An arrow with "Hey, down here!" written in blue neon announcing the recent use of the entrance would hardly have been more noticeable. Any trained scientist—even one who'd rather dissect than observe—would be curious.

"I am a double idiot *jerk*," moaned Salt. He turned off the flashlight and listened. All was silent except the faint echoing whir of a sports utility backing up over coal grit. "I led you guys straight into a blind alley. There's no way out. We're trapped!"

Rascal, stretched out across Salt's boots, rattled his wings. Even in his horrible panic, Salt noted Rascal's behavior. A whole-body twitch characteristic of an irritated dragon. Boy, if Rascal could speak: "Pipe down, willya, kid? Some of us have slithered our tails off today."

The tiny part of Salt's brain that wasn't paralyzed with fear thought about Rascal's behavior. Interesting. The dragon in Dr. Zhao's video—the one with the vicious tail swipe—had rattled his wings just like that a couple of seconds before he took that poke at Dr. Zhao. Salt had seen it a hundred times. Twitch. Rattle. Swipe. Good thing Dr. Zhao had jumped out of the way. Bet those tail spikes could really do some serious damage.

"Bet they could," murmured Salt, full of a brilliant plan.

He crouched in front of the great wooden door until his head was in line with the iron padlock. Rascal was already pretty irritable. A loud human voice would

certainly provoke a tail swipe. Salt took a deep breath—
and out popped the words of the loud human voice
nearest and dearest to his heart—the incredible words of
Allison Fishbinder:

"It's not your *hands,* Salt.
It's your *hair.*
It's your *shirt.*
It's your *shoes.*
You're gonna stink up the whole—"

That did it. Rascal's tail spike lashed out.

No fancy jump out of the way for Salt, no sir. He dove
for the dirt as Rascal's tail cracked through the air. The
spikes swiped the space where his head had been just
seconds ago and crashed dead on into the padlock. As
the sound of a big motor revving up hard for the final
descent came echoing from above, the brittle padlock
exploded into a thousand pieces. Splintery iron thumb-
tacks rained down upon Salt's head, upon the dragons'
heads, upon the ground, upon everything. The iron
chain slithered out of the hinge. And the wooden doors
creaked slowly inward.

The dragons raised their snouts and flicked their
tongues, tasting the wonderful smell of pure underground.

"Nice shot, Rascal," said Salt. He tore off his parka and wrapped it around his right forearm. "Okay everybody—over the edge!"

Using the toes of his boots and his jacket-protected arm, he scrambled over the lip of the mine shaft. The second his body went over the edge, his boots hit nothing but air. Salt realized that he should have looked before he leaped.

"YIKES!"

He grabbed wildly for Rascal's tail spikes, missed, and disappeared over the edge.

For one scary moment, he fell through thin air. The inclined tunnel rushed up to meet him, and Salt rolled down a slope of loose rock and debris, totally out of control, two hundred feet in less than thirty seconds. He landed with a thump on a shale outcropping that functioned as the roof overhang of a tunnel branching off the main shaft.

Panting, he rolled over, found his flashlight, and turned it on. Sure enough, the dragons were slithering after him, single file, undulating in a stately and dignified manner over the lip of earth, down the seamed and pitted walls.

"C'mon guys, move it, move it," muttered Salt.

Smokey, the runt of the litter, inched over the edge. Pal and Queenie reached Salt's rock ledge. Queenie

169

bumped the flashlight with her snout. Pal twined around his legs. Slowly, deliberately, the rest of the pack descended.

Salt crossed his fingers and prayed. They were gonna make it, they were gonna make it. They were gonna—

Overhead the rock wall glowed dimly, then brightened under the intense white beams of a pair of halogen headlights. As Aunt Mary Athena gunned the engine, the Rover shrieked down the iron rails. Salt could hear the Rover's back end fishtailing into the rock walls under his aunt's lead foot.

Salt cut off his flashlight. "Down! Sit! Stay!" he hissed, willing the dragons to behave for once. Incredibly, unbelievably, the six dragons still crawling down the mine shaft froze in midundulation. Heads down, wings folded neatly, the dragons clung to the rocky slope. Awaiting further orders.

Salt blinked, astonished.

A set of antilock brakes screeched to a halt overhead; four tires kicked up a huge cloud of coal dust. Headlights pierced the dingy haze, illuminating the entrance into the shaft. Salt could just make out Smokey's grimy red tail spikes, a mere five feet below the edge, bristling against the black rock. Uh-oh.

He heard his aunt pull the emergency brake. The Rover's engine dieseled loudly, overheated from a long afternoon of dragon hunting. The car door banged open. Aunt Mary Athena, cursing and muttering, got out.

She crossed in front of the headlights, a tall, black figure crunching through the coal grit in high-heeled alligator boots. Her shadow, backlit by the high beams, obscured by dust, fell over the edge of the underground mine and melted into the darkness below. Silence.

Salt panicked. He shoved closer to the rock wall. Pal, dozing across his knees, shoved back. Salt clung to Pal and prayed with all his might that his aunt was really, truly, and deeply a research scientist of action, someone who'd rather cut something up than stare blankly into a big black hole in the ground and think about stuff. Because if she looked down and noticed Smokey's tail spikes sticking out of the rock wall, they were goners.

"Everywhere I go, it's nothing but dust, dirt, and more dust," complained Aunt Mary Athena. "I cannot see a *thing* in this light." Her voice sounded dry and rustling, like something slithering through the grass.

His aunt coughed. Salt cowered against Pal, his heart thumping in his ears. She coughed again. All eight dragons raised their heads, suddenly alert. Queenie hissed softly. The rest of the dragons hissed back. The alligator boots crunched closer to the edge of the shaft.

"What was that?" she demanded. Her voice carried ringingly over the Rover's dieseling chug. "Some animal or something?" Salt about had a heart attack.

Dragonic fire—a heatless blue flame chemically related to the "cold" electricity produced by lightning bugs—flickered from Queenie's nostrils and curled along her jaw. Salt reached over and clamped his fingers around her snout.

"Bad girl," he breathed in her ear folds. "Stop that."

Queenie quivered under his hand, yearning to answer his aunt. Despite his terror, Salt stared at the alpha female, puzzled. Just that morning at the wheyr, the dragons had slunk away, spooked by the sound of his aunt's voice. And now they were attracted? It didn't make sense.

"Salt? Are you there? I am looking for you."

Astonished, Salt stared up through the gloom of the tunnel. Him? She was looking for *him* all of a sudden? That really didn't make sense. What was going on?

Queenie opened her jaws and grunted. Salt grabbed her snout with both hands. She tried to jerk away. Under the low throb of the Rover's engine, Salt silently wrestled her jaws into a hammerlock.

"No," breathed Salt into her ear folds. "We don't give up. We never give up."

Boy. That was stupid coming from him. What kind of guy was he to hand out hero advice, anyway? There he was, dirty and scared and dizzy with hunger. Hiding out in a great big hole in the ground, too chicken to face down his aunt. Hoping she'd just go away. Hoping the dragons would just kept quiet. Praying he wouldn't give in and start whimpering.

Queenie went limp in his arms, snuggling into his body heat. He hugged the dragon's head to his chest, felt the weight of her, smelled her sulphurous dragonstink, listened to the pull of air whistling through her fire-breather's nostrils. He dropped his head and rubbed his chin against her dry, abrasive head scales. Queenie rumbled in contentment.

Salt's throat tightened. No way. No way was he going to let his aunt lay so much as one pointy fingernail on a single snout. If she climbed down the shaft, he'd . . . he'd bean her with his flashlight! Tie her up with the belt from his tool kit! The dragons would hiss and snarl like ferocious watchdogs while he hiked back to Spratt and called out the National Guard!

It didn't matter how scared he was—and he was plenty scared. It didn't matter how weak he was—and boy, his arms felt yanked out of the sockets. It didn't matter how trapped he was—and halfway down a mine shaft was pretty doggone trapped. Salt knew what he was going to do. He was going to protect the dragons, dead—Salt gulped, remembering the chain saw—or alive.

Nervously, he looked up, hoping his aunt wasn't on her way down with her chain saw. She wasn't. Aunt Mary Athena stood and stared not down the mine shaft, thank goodness, but at her hands held out in front of her. The weird shadows cast by the Rover's headlights made her fingers seem extra long, her arms extra short. The black sleeves of her shirt hung baggy at the elbows. But the neck zipper had been stretched sideways until the teeth had pulled away in the middle. One dry and scaly-looking shoulder peeked through the gap.

Aunt Mary Athena cleared her throat and rasped, "What the heck is happening to my *hands*?"

Salt craned his neck, trying to get a better look. His aunt waggled her fingers, then curved them into claws. The shadows danced crazily.

"Good Lord. The side effects of this experiment are totally unacceptable," she muttered as she stalked back to the Range Rover. "I need more data. The lab computer ought to be finished running the statistical model. And I need my eight o'clock tree bark supplements." The heel of her boot knocked a couple of iron splinters over the edge. They plinked, planked, plonked all the way to the bottom far, far below. A car door slammed. Aunt Mary Athena threw the Range Rover into gear and the vehicle screamed up the mule track. In reverse.

Salt raised his head. He listened to the Rover bounce

onto the access road and zoom off into the night. Back the same way it had come.

Salt raised his head a little more. "Did you hear that?" he said, awestruck, to the dragons. "Aunt Mary Athena gave up! She's gone back to her lab! Man, we are *saved*!"

Salt grabbed Pal's tail spikes in a victory hug. The dragon woke up with a snort. "Okay, it wasn't a major save, and it had a huge element of luck, but *man*!" Salt raised his fists high above his head. "I thought we were dead meat. Score one for the good guys!"

Salt lowered his arms. His eyes were shining as the pack caterpillared down to the ledge. The dragons just about trampled each other trying to get up close, right next to him. John Salt, rescuer of dragons.

He stood there for a moment, basking in glory as the dragons clustered around him, flicking tongues over his hands, rubbing a spit shine onto the steel buckle of his tool belt. He couldn't believe it. He'd done it. He had done something pretty brave even though he had been scared out of his mind. Salt rubbed his sore shoulders. The pain was a badge of courage. Who would have thought? Maybe this hero stuff would actually work out for him.

Coolly, casually, Salt turned on his flashlight and aimed the beam over the edge of the shale outcropping, down, down, down into the shaft.

"That way, men," he said in a deep, sure voice, gesturing into the blackness. "You're safe now, thanks to me." For a second he imagined the great Dr. Zhao himself pinning a glittering medal on his parka. Warmly shaking his hand. Congratulating him on a job well done.

Salt grinned. Boy. If only Allison Fishbinder could see him now.

Chapter Fourteen

B oy. It was really starting to bug her, the thing Dr. Salt had about her nephew's DNA. Candi chewed up a whole pack of gum almost, thinking about it. And the more she thought about it, the weirder her thinking got. Nah. Couldn't be. And yet . . .

Only thing to do was find Salt and make sure he was okay.

That turned out to be the trick, finding Salt. Candi biked out to the wheyr and hung around for a while, but he never showed. And he hadn't been to his house to feed Loretta. By the time Candi coasted back up the Salts' driveway on her bike, the smelly buzzard kicked up such a hungry fuss that Candi dug a package of frozen mice out of the bottom of the garage freezer and poked their tiny corpses through the wire mesh with the tip of her index finger. Ew. Ew. Ew.

Finally, Candi gave up, rode home, and got yelled at for staying out past nine o'clock. She sulked in her bedroom until midnight, when she snuck downstairs and called Grandma's.

"Hi, Grandma! How're you—I know it's really late—of *course* they don't know I'm on the phone, why do you think I'm whispering—if you just lemme talk to Ham a minute, I'll hang right up, I swear!"

"Grandma's mad," yawned Ham into the phone.

"Forget Grandma. Listen, Ham, did Salt go to your ball game in Sarahsville?"

"Salt? Why would he do that? He hates baseball. He even refuses to watch that Hall of Fame video he got for Christmas. It's pretty good. There's this one part where—"

"Will you shut up a minute? You got no idea where Salt is?"

"Well, he's with those dragons, wherever they are. I can guarantee you that."

Candi slammed the phone down. Hard.

"For cryin' out loud, Candi!" moaned her dad from his bedroom.

Hmm. How was she going to find John Salt and nine—oops, eight—stupid dragons before Dr. Salt did?

Candi trudged up the stairs. She kicked off her shoes and stretched out on her bed. Starlight glimmered on a poster of Marie Antoinette checking out her eye makeup in the Hall of Mirrors. So what *was* the deal with Dr. Salt and her nephew's DNA? Candi yawned. She closed her eyes. And fell asleep.

Just before dawn, Candi had a dream. She dreamed she was flying over Paris, France, all pale and perfect and dressed in black when her pale, perfect face began to crack and fall off, revealing a bald-headed, one-eyed turkey buzzard beneath her makeup. The buzzard started to fall out of the sky, straight toward the spiky steel point of the Eiffel Tower. Candi flapped her arms harder—and fell out of bed.

Dizzily, she put a hand to her face. Shoot. She had fallen asleep wearing all that makeup. She dragged herself into the bathroom. She locked the door and slowly unwrapped the last, limp piece of gum from her pocket. Her hand froze halfway to her mouth.

"Of *course* it was not a superficial change to the upper dermatological layers. It was an alteration to the very molecular structure of the skin cells. Basic protein strands fused with the dragonic—"

Okay. So Dr. Salt had managed to fuse her human DNA with that dead dragon's, Blackie, or whoever, and invented a surefire wrinkle cream that got rid of your wrinkles, but turned your skin green and scaly. And then your hair fell out. Maybe you could wear a ton of liquid foundation and keep your hat on, but frankly, it was hard to imagine very many people going for it.

Candi stuck the piece of gum into her mouth and stared deeply into the mirror.

Okay. So if that dragon's DNA really did alter the very molecular structure of her skin, the body's largest organ, then it was definitely replicating throughout Dr. Salt's body. After a couple of days, all the matte pancake on the planet wasn't gonna be able to cover up a systemic change like that. No doubt about it. Dr. Mary Athena Salt, longtime role model in the high-powered world of professional beauty, was no longer human. She was morphing into . . .

"A dragon," Candi whispered to her reflection. "Boy, oh boy, oh boy."

And Dr. Salt knew she'd be stuck as a snake forever (okay, with ten-foot wings, but still) unless she could reverse the process. Hmm. A fresh infusion of human protein complexes in a hemoglobin base would probably do it. Course, not just any human DNA, and not just any hemoglobin base. It'd have to be genetically related DNA, and a compatible blood type. Like from a twerpy nephew or something.

Candi inhaled sharply and swallowed her gum. "Jeez, Salt!" she wheezed, "Your aunt is *really* out to get you."

She gulped down a glass of water and patted her

chest until she stopped coughing. Then she ran hot water over her washrag. The question was, How to prevent more murder and mayhem? Ham was a dope, but he had a point. Salt would be with those dragons, that's for sure. Dead—Candi gulped, remembering the hacksaw and hand drill peeking out of Dr. Salt's toolbox—or alive.

But how was she supposed to find the dragons? Jeez, it was so frustrating to be stuck in the bathroom at five o'clock in the morning, scraping off a bunch of disgusting, slept-on makeup, when really she ought to be sailing above the Wilds like she had in the Paris of her dreams, soaring over slag heaps and holding ponds and abandoned mine shafts, swooping under high-tension wires, flapping 'round and 'round the forgotten quarry roads, homing in on . . .

"That's it," breathed Candi.

She dropped the makeup-smeared washrag onto the counter and turned to go. She caught a glimpse of her fresh-scrubbed face in the mirror and stopped.

"Ever since Dr. Salt came to Spratt, I've denied myself all the pleasures of color. Well, forget that, huh?" she said.

Her hand reached out and closed upon her absolute favorite rhinestone hair clips, sparkly pink dragonflies. Gleefully, she stuck every single clip into her hairdo.

Okay, it was overdone, tacky even, but who cared? She sure didn't. Did. Not. Care. She loved color. She leaned forward and examined her face in the mirror, turning her head from side to side. Hey, this was the *real* Candi Clarke—pretty, popular, and why not finally admit it? smart—looking back at her.

"René Descartes was right," she murmured. "He said you shouldn't accept anything as true unless it presents itself so clearly and distinctly that you have no occasion to doubt it. And the truth is, pink is such a *great* color. How could I have ever doubted?"

Candi blew a kiss at the mirror, threw on her platform sneakers, and clattered downstairs, full of her brilliant plan. The perfect plan that would not only find Salt and the dragons, but really, really stick one to Dr. Mary Athena Salt.

She hopped on her bike and pedaled over to the Salts' house. Nobody was home, of course, what with Salt hiding and his folks still in Washington. Candi peeked through a few windows just to be sure. Nope. Nobody home.

Nobody but Loretta. Candi stood on the back porch and smirked. So Ham thought he was being witty calling her Birdbrain, huh? Some birds were pretty darned smart. Some birds went after what they wanted. Take Loretta, for instance. Loretta, the one-eyed turkey

182

buzzard, who followed those dragons around like a starry-eyed preteen following around a sophisticated director of Research and Development, who—

"Honestly, I don't know what I was thinking. The woman has gone off the deep end," Candi said to Loretta as she opened the cage door. "Phew. What have you been eating, girl? Not to mention ruthless and conniving. And does she ever wear anything the least bit *fun*?"

With a great swirl of rusty black wings, Loretta hopped out of the cage and took off.

"You know something?" Candi murmured grimly as she hopped on her bike and pedaled after Loretta. "I'm beginning to wonder if Paris is worth it."

Chapter Fifteen

After a couple of tries, John Salt finally hauled himself over the edge of the mine shaft. The dragons were underground. Safe—for now. But Aunt Mary Athena would never give up looking. He still had work to do.

A soft, rumbling snore echoed faintly out of the tunnel. That sweet, homey sound made Salt feel every sore muscle and every aching bone. Wearily, he looked up at the slice of starry night sky above the canyon walls, looking for the north star. Boy, what a day. And it wasn't over yet. Spratt and the nearest phone were a five-mile hike away.

Good grief.

Salt dragged himself up the mule track and trudged northward. Though his dead-tired legs and empty stomach were mighty distracting, Salt puzzled over Aunt Mary

Athena's murderous obsession with the dragons. An hour and a half later, trying not to jump at every spooky night sound, Salt was pretty sure he had figured it out. His aunt had applied the scientific method to myth and discovered a fascinating fact. Dragonblood made you immortal.

Well—almost immortal. Dragons lived a thousand years, never growing old or feeble, simply enjoying the endless years of young dragonhood. Maturity and reproduction, which happened very late in the dragonic life cycle, were followed shortly by death. Since Aunt Mary Athena had never seemed all that interested in reproducing in the first place, she had a real shot at immortality.

Forever young. Aunt Mary Athena would jump at that, absolutely.

Despite the chilly night air, Salt began to sweat. The wrinkle creme of immortality. The face-lift of the gods. Everybody would want it. But greedy Aunt Mary Athena would hoard the supply. Each tiny jar would cost a fortune. Not that cost would matter. Movie stars would line up to pay. Football players would list *wrinkle creme* as their top demand during contract talks. Even the president of the United States would sign over a big chunk of the Social Security budget to Aunt Mary Athena in order to regain the firm jaw and steely-eyed gaze of a world leader in the prime of life.

But the madness wouldn't end with the rich and famous. Would fun-loving old Uncle Dinsmore want to buy a wrinkle creme guaranteed to make him look twenty years old again? Absolutely. And what would he do to get it? Pawn his custom-made toilet wrench? Sell his car?

"Rob a bank?" Salt muttered.

Bank bank rob a bank? echoed the slag heaps all around. Salt pictured Uncle Dinsmore with a ski mask and a gun making a break for the getaway car. It wasn't all that hard to imagine, actually. That thought made him shiver.

Aunt Mary Athena's wrinkle creme would cause nothing but anarchy and heartbreak. The total breakdown of civilization. Fortunately, he, John Salt, was right on top of stuff, foiling his aunt's evil plans. Like a hero, maybe.

"Like a hero for sure," panted Salt as he pushed through the shifting rockfall between two hills. "Allison Fishbinder is gonna flip when she hears."

Salt got so wrapped up in daydreaming about Allison Fishbinder that he forgot to check the stars. Away he drifted eastward. When he topped the last hill of rock and mess, he saw the line of moonlit grass running beneath a barbed-wire fence. Six southern white rhino, gray hills in the starlight, slept just beyond the fence.

"Yes!" cried Salt.

He knew exactly where he was. The South African veldts. If he backtracked a little, he could cut through the woods behind Ham's house, beg a slice or two of butterscotch almond log from Mrs. Clarke, then call his parents in Washington and tell them to catch the next plane home. End of the adventure.

Salt rubbed his eyes and yawned. Sure, it had been exciting, a thrill and a challenge and all that, but frankly, he was beat. And his feet were killing him.

He turned north and jogged down the hill. At the bottom he tripped into a washout, stumbled, and almost hit the dirt. He staggered a few steps and then totally lost his balance—because the ground was moving. With a queer rattle, the grass collapsed under his feet. And Salt fell into a hole.

He careened down to the bottom on the seat of his pants, scraping his palms open as he tried to keep himself from rolling. The pit opened up into an old room-and-pillar chamber, a coal seam excavation forty feet across and ten feet high with support pillars of coal still holding up the overburdened roof. Salt hit the bedrock with a bang. He threw his arms over his head to protect his skull from the ton and a half of grass, dirt, and rock that rattled down after him.

A slab of shale tipped over the edge. It whooshed past

his ear and smacked his right kneecap before skidding across his leg, pinning it to the ground. Salt yelped in pain.

It was all over in less than a minute. The avalanche subsided to a thin trickle of sifting dirt. Cautiously, Salt pulled his arms away from his head. He pulled up the neck of his sweatshirt and covered his nose and mouth against the mushroom cloud of coal dust rising through the air. He squinted into the gloom as he felt along the edge of the slab across his leg.

It was some big rock. Two hundred pounds, easy, that had missed his head by an inch. Salt took a deep, grateful breath—and winced. There he lay, pinned by the shin bone to the bottom of a forty-foot sinkhole; cold, filthy, and unspeakably hungry. His ankle seemed okay. But his knee felt funny.

Good grief. Falling into a hole. Pitiful. Pitiful, strutting around dreaming about being the hero who got the girl in the end and not paying attention to where he was putting his stupid feet. What an idiot. At daybreak the dragons would go aboveground and lounge around, waiting for Salt to show up with a Holstein. They'd be sitting ducks.

What a jerk, strutting around thinking he was saving the dragons. A couple of hot tears trickled into his grimy ears. And then a couple more. Salt looked blindly up through the little skyhole at the stars overhead. The Milky Way looked close enough to touch.

He lay flat on his back, sniveling. Okay. Okay. Things were pretty grim. Not only had he failed the dragons, but he had failed himself. The furthest thing from a hero you could imagine. Good thing this looked like . . . the end. Because if he could sink any lower, he sure didn't want to know about it.

Salt hunched into his jacket. His life tried to flash before his eyes—but instead of baby pictures, Salt saw the dragons instead.

Everything they'd seen together, all the things they'd done. Endless, lazy days soaking up the afternoon sun outside the wheyr. The long, nervous stare Smokey had given his first bullfrog. The sight of Pal stretched out along the top branch of the largest climbing tree in the dragons' pasture. The weight of Queenie's snout in his hammerlock.

Salt raised his bone-cold hands and swiped at the wet on his face. He didn't want to give up. More to the point, he *couldn't* give up, even if he wanted to. Because this whole thing wasn't about him, John Salt. It had never been about him, about his dreams of greatness and heroes and girls and gold medals. It was about something much bigger—about something more wonderful, about something far finer than whether plain old John Salt lived or . . . you know.

It was about the dragons.

"You're the greatest thing that ever happened to me," he whispered—and a bit of courage stirred in his heart.

He took a deep breath, wiped his face one last time, and lay still, planning his next move. There wasn't much to plan. Conserve body heat. Endure the night. Groaning, he lifted his shoulders a little, flipped the hood of his parka over his head, and tied it firmly under his chin. He fumbled with the work gloves in his pocket and put them on. Daybreak was a long time from now.

But he'd tough it out, somehow. He wasn't that far from a loop of road that the animal techs used to haul feed out to the rhinos every morning. Come daybreak he'd start yelling. He'd yell and yell. He'd throw rocks far enough out of the sinkhole so they wouldn't roll back and bonk him on the head. Or he'd shove that rock across his leg out of the way, just *shove* it, and out he'd crawl, crawl as far as he had to because Aunt Mary Athena was still on the loose and the dragons weren't safe, no sir, and he'd never give up. Never. Never, never, never.

He pulled his elbows out of his parka sleeves and wrapped his arms around his chest. Conserve body heat.

Endure the night. Wearily, he closed his eyes.

Just before dawn, Salt had a dream. He dreamed that the dragons had mesquite grilled a Holstein and were beckoning him and Allison Fishbinder to the feast. Salt licked his lips and smiled.

Chapter Sixteen

—꧅—

Loretta, the red-necked turkey buzzard, bobbed and wove and fell out of the sky while Candi followed on her bike. They traveled through the Wilds and onto unreclaimed coal lands.

Candi rubbed her eyes and yawned. Maybe this hadn't been such a hot idea after all. Loretta hadn't quite got the hang of one-eyed flying yet. She'd flap her wings for twenty, thirty feet maybe, then list suddenly to the left and crash into the ground. She'd stagger to her little birdy feet and try again. Stop and start. Stop and start. They were getting nowhere, fast.

The sky grew lighter. The buzzard flew above an access road winding through the barren landscape. Candi biked past an open gate with a sign that read:

**WARNING
UNDERGROUND MINE AREA
PROCEED WITH EXTREME CAUTION
WEIGHT LIMITS STRICTLY ENFORCED**

Candi shuddered. After a few minutes of hard pedaling, she looked up and saw Loretta sail off to the left, over the trees, away from the road.

She almost missed the trail that sloped between the bushes. Her bike rattled along a set of munchkin-sized train tracks as the walls closed in and Loretta circled overhead. The buzzard swooped low between the canyon walls and coasted in for a landing. She bounced twice, stretched out her neck, and strutted the last twenty feet to the gaping mouth of an old underground mine. Candi got off her bike, crunched through a bunch of splintery iron chips, and peered past the old wooden doors standing ajar. A cold, damp sulphur wind whistled past her face.

"Shoot," said Candi. "I forgot the hot dogs."

It didn't matter. As soon as the dragons heard her voice, they began to slither out of the hole.

"Arright you guys," said Candi. She reached into her bicycle basket and dug out Salt's old, incredibly filthy, size-ten boot, which she had found in Loretta's bone pile on Salt's back porch. The shoelaces were chewed to ribbons, the metal eyelets totally gone. She held out the boot between her thumb and forefinger and breathed through her mouth.

"Ew. Smell thad? Good and stinky? Smells just like Sald, huh? Okay, dragons. Fetch!"

One of the dragons, a big, greenish-goldish thing with an incredibly bored expression on its face, reared back and clapped its wings.

"Hey! My hair!" yelped Candi. She dropped Salt's boot and threw her hands over her hairdo.

The dragons caterpillared off. By the time Candi had smoothed her pink rhinestone hair clips back into place and got her bangs to behave, the dragons had slithered up the tracks and nearly out of sight. Fortunately, Loretta wobbled in the sky above them, marking their progress.

With a deep, heartfelt sigh, Candi pushed her bike up the train tracks and onto the dirt road. She swung onto her bike seat. The dragons, far ahead, were heading cross-country, crawling in a wide arc to the northeast. They reared up every once in a while to flap their wings—*wak, wak, wak*, a really annoying sound, like two old drumsticks banging—and then dropped down to slither faster than before. Candi fell farther and farther behind.

"Stupid dragons," she panted.

She couldn't see them anymore, but she could hear them *wak*king away, along with some weird thumps and bumps that reminded her of Loretta's crash landings. It was getting hard to follow them. Okay, so first their belly trails would be in a clear, snakey unbroken line. Then the trails would disappear. After fifty yards of nothing, suddenly there'd be another eight squiggly depressions, eight slithery tracks.

"What in the world are those stupid dragons doing?" muttered Candi. "Hopping?"

She ground up the steepest hill yet and stopped. Six southern white rhinos were lined up along the Wilds' barbed-wire fence, sniffing anxiously in the direction of eight dragons milling around the lip of a forty-foot sinkhole. One of the rhinos hooted nervously. Eight reptile necks whipped around, eight alert snouts pointed toward the quarry. In a flash the rhinos were thundering toward West Africa, the dragons in hot pursuit.

Candi climbed down the hill. She stood at the sinkhole's edge. It was totally dark down there, totally grassy up here, and not a sign of Salt anywhere.

"Phooey," she said. "Ditched by those stupid dragons. Now how am I supposed to find him?"

Dead silence. Then she heard Salt's voice murmuring, "Allison? Allison, is that you?"

Chapter Seventeen

—⁂—

"Good grief, Salt, what are you, delirious? Allison Fishbinder wouldn't be caught dead out here! It's me, Candi Clarke!"

Salt opened his eyes. He must be dreaming. Candi Clarke was the last person on earth he expected to see. Yet there she stood, big as life, rolling her eyes at him from the edge of the sinkhole. The soft light of dawn glimmered on a bunch of sparkly hair things stuck in her frizzy brown hair. It gave her a pink halo.

She knelt and knocked a dirt clod loose. It toppled over and clunked him right on the head.

"Ow!"

"Boy, oh boy, oh boy, Salt. Are you okay?"

Salt grimaced. "No, I'm not okay! I'm trapped and starving and I had to *walk* five miles yesterday and—"

"Huh? I can barely hear you!"

Salt was filled with despair. This was going to be a terrible rescue. Of all the people in the world to wander by, why did it have to be Candi Clarke? Ham called her Birdbrain. For very good reasons. Unfortunately. He'd have to use words of one syllable.

"Candi. Here's the deal. MY LEG IS PINNED BY A REAL BIG ROCK. I CAN'T GET OUT. I NEED HELP."

"Oh wow. I better go for help, huh?"

"No, wait!" cried Salt. "You gotta call my parents in Washington first and tell them to come straight home! The dragons are in terrible danger!"

"What?"

"I SAID—"

"Jeez, I can't hear a thing you're saying. It's all echoey and stuff. Wait a sec. I'm coming down."

Relief swept through him. Candi was climbing down. Candi was going to help. Salt squinched his eyes shut, grateful. From now on he'd be Candi's new best friend. He'd convince Ham to stop calling her Birdbrain. He'd kiss her feet, let her copy his homework—anything.

"Just hurry," whimpered Salt.

Candi jumped down. "Jeez, it smells funny down here," she said, wiping her dirty hands on her jeans. "Dark, too. I can hardly see you."

She examined the rock pinning Salt's leg to the ground. "Well, this isn't such a big deal, Salt," she said.

197

"All we need is a little leverage." She climbed out of the sinkhole and climbed back in, lugging a broken tree branch. She wedged the branch under the rock slab and lifted it off Salt's knee.

"OW!"

"Hey, your leg looks okay, but lookit your knee. See, right there through the rip in your jeans? Ew. It is the most disgusting mix of teal and lavender with melon undertones that I have ever seen. Doesn't look broken, though. Sprained, maybe. Well. Never mind that."

She grabbed the front of his parka, yanked him to his feet, and steadied him against the rock wall. "I have been looking all over for you, Salt. Now, you know about your aunt, right?"

Salt shook off her grabby little hands and tried to clear his head of pain, hunger, and the up-close smell of Candi's weird perfume.

"Yeah, I know. My evil aunt has perfected the secret formula for her wrinkle creme. Dragonblood. Keeps you looking young for about a thousand years."

Candi popped her gum thoughtfully. "A thousand years. No kidding, huh? And it works great, except for that one pesky side effect. Your aunt fused her human DNA strands with that dragon she—you know."

Salt gasped. "You mean—?"

Candi nodded. "Dr. Salt is half human, half dragon.

And the nastiest half of both, in my opinion. Though not for long. She'll be full dragon before breakfast time."

Salt's stomach growled hopefully at the word *breakfast*, but he ignored it. He took a few practice steps, wondering if his knee would hold out for the climb. "We have to get out of here. The dragons—"

Candi snorted. "Forget the dragons, Salt. You're the one who's in big trouble here. See, your aunt's figured out how to reverse the process and regain her human nature—and with her, I'm using the term loosely. All she needs is a whole lotta untainted human DNA from somebody who's a close genetic match. A relative. Like, oh, say, a twerpy nephew?"

Salt stared at her, thunderstruck. "You mean—"

"You know what she did to Blackie, or whoever, right?"

Salt nodded sadly.

"Well then. To her it's a simple case of nephew sacrifice for the greater good of a guaranteed skin care regime."

"But," squeaked Salt. He cleared his throat. "I'm a guy," he said in a semiregular voice, "I have guy DNA. She'd grow a mustache—eventually, I mean, when my blood serum hits puberty."

"Nah, Salt. I know what I'm talking about here. Not to brag or anything, but I did get an A plus on the evolutionary biology midterm. Trust me, we're dealing with compatibility factors here. Dr. Salt has no female relatives. No *blood* female relatives, if you get my meaning. She'll make do with you."

Salt's jaw dropped. "You got an A plus on the evolutionary biology midterm?"

Candi waved her hands impatiently. "Get used to it, Salt. I'm smart—smart enough to be sick and tired of acting cute and perky and slightly dumb all the time. Which is totally beside the point. The point is, your aunt is out to get you. And if we don't stop her, you are dead meat."

Loretta crash-landed onto Salt's shoulder and poked through several of his pockets, looking for dead meat.

A dark shadow crept over the sinkhole, blotting out the pale sky of dawn. Something heavy and slow humped to the lip of the sinkhole forty feet above their heads. And it spoke.

"Sssssssalt? Are yew thaire?"

The dark shape reared up, towered over the sinkhole. The last few stars still on the horizon glimmered faintly through the shape's tattered black designer outfit, glimmered on the rope of pearls still twined around its neck.

"Sssssssalt? I know yew are thaire. Heire is a bike, heire are the dragons. And I smell yuowr ssscent on the aire. Yissss. I yam coming down to find yew."

"Holy smokes," yelped Salt.

Candi had been right about his aunt. Aunt Mary Athena was crawling down the side of the hole head-first. Her neck had fused into her torso. She gripped the rocks with her stubby green forearms and three-fingered hands, her legs curving sinuously over the rock ledges. She must have lost her alligator boots when her feet formed the short tail ridged with a bristly row of crimson spikes characteristic of adult dragons. The handle of her toolbox was wedged between her slightly open jaws.

She reached the bottom of the hole and spat out the toolbox. "Yew see how I yam desperate. I have perhaps an hour left only." She undulated toward him, a jumbo-sized bone saw held clumsily between her misshapen hand stubs. "Yew see?"

A huge jolt of adrenaline shot through Salt. The pain from his knee was totally forgotten as an urgent message radioed from the most primitive part of Salt's brain stem: "Excuse me, but she is gonna *cut off your head*! *Flight!*

"No," said Salt. "We won't run. Not anymore."

"Oh sure, like we got someplace to run to down here!" screeched Candi. "We're trapped! Do something, Salt! She's *your* aunt!"

FIGHT?

Fight? Well, no, not that either. Sure, a regular hero would charge Aunt Mary Athena, braving hand-to-stub combat, crashing into walls and breaking up the rocks. But if Salt had learned anything from this whole uncomfortable adventure, it was that galloping head-long to the rescue was not his style. He was way more laid-back than that.

Salt's eyes narrowed. He wasn't a hero, not really. Just . . . brave, sort of. Smart, even though his evolutionary biology midterm had come back with a big fat C minus scrawled across the top. But one of the good guys, definitely. And a good guy with a couple of tricks still up his sleeve.

Or tool belt, to be precise. Salt's fingers closed upon his trusty flashlight.

"Candi," he whispered urgently, "give me one of your hair things."

"One of my— Salt, are you insane? Who *cares* about hairstyles right now! We're gonna die!"

"Nobody's going to die," he said as he leaned over and ripped out the shiny pink hair thing over Candi's left ear. "At least, I don't think so."

"Ow! That *hurt*!"

Loretta squawked irritably and flew off his shoulder to perch on a rockfall.

"Now watch," Salt said. "Watch this."

202

He held up the hair thing. A strand of Candi's brown frizzy hair tickled his fingers, but he ignored that, concentrating on the most basic of dragonic behaviors. Dragons loved shiny objects. His aunt, whose regular human nature craved the shiny, the shallow, and the superficial, was sure to be more attracted than most. And here they were, trapped underground with one of the shiniest, shallowest objects in the universe: a cheap, pink rhinestone hair clip.

Salt trained the flashlight on the rhinestones. A hundred shiny lights sprang out from the faceted surfaces. A pink rainbow shimmered in the damp air between the hair thing and the rock wall. Salt twirled his fingers. Pink diamonds spangled and sparkled over his face, his hands, Aunt Mary Athena's snout, everywhere. Mineral deposits from water erosion in the rock face behind him—pink and purple and red—glinted back until the very air twinkled and shimmered and glowed. Salt grinned. A little heat, a little light, a whole lotta shine. Irresistible. Sure enough, Aunt Mary Athena stopped, transfixed.

"Whoa. Great idea, Salt," muttered Candi, wide-eyed, at his shoulder. "You distract the dragon lady while I sneak up from behind." She punched his arm and disappeared into the shadows.

"Pretty, how prrretty," Aunt Mary Athena murmured

as she leaned toward the light, her head swaying slowly. Salt limped off to the left.

"I luff the pink light, don't yew?" hummed Aunt Mary Athena. A cold, blue flame streaked along her jaw, then disappeared. "Warm, so warm. All the pretty sparkly jewellsss. And my nephiew. Oh, yissss. My nephiew, John Ssssssalt."

His aunt rippled out of the shadows, greed and desire mingled plainly in her expression of triumph. The pink light burnished each snaggle-toothed edge of the bone saw that she held, limp and forgotten, between her stubs.

Salt felt powerful, in control, as he led his aunt slowly along the outer edge of the rock face. Yep, totally collected and cool and in control—until he realized his aunt was a whole lot faster on undulating belly than he was on sprained kneecap.

She was gaining on him.

Salt limped a little faster. Hot, snaky breath whiffled through the top of his hair. His aunt, mesmerized, unblinking, towered over him. Salt broke into a hobble. Maybe this wasn't such a hot idea after all.

"Uh, Candi?" Vainly, Salt tried to peer around his aunt. "Anytime now, Candi. Candi?"

Good grief. She hadn't climbed out of the sinkhole while the climbing was good, had she?

"Candi, honest, I could use a little help here."

Dead silence.

Candi Clarke had finked out on him. Well, he wasn't a bit surprised. And now it was rapidly coming down to a fight. Salt hadn't been in a fistfight since third grade, when Randall Wright had punched him in the stomach during recess. Before Salt could punch back, Randall had laughed and run away.

Salt gritted his teeth. Well, he had done a lot of stuff lately that he'd never thought he could do. Rescue dragons. Outwit his aunt. Miss a bunch of meals. Trust Candi to sneak up from behind. He might as well try a frontal attack. Ham always said the best defense was a good offense. Or was it the other way around? Salt hoped Ham knew what he was talking about.

Salt dropped Candi-the-Traitor's pink hair thing. Good riddance. He swung the flashlight beam square into his aunt's face, aiming for the lidless eye closest to him. Like a thousand burning knives, the white light stabbed at her unprotected retina. Aunt Mary Athena reared back, howling in pain. Salt ducked under the wavering bone saw and limped off as fast as he could.

The spell was broken. Aunt Mary Athena shook herself angrily.

"What have yew done to mee?" she roared. She raised the bone saw high and peered around, still half blinded. "Wee will finush it now!"

A rock flew out of the darkness, clanged off the bone saw, and ricocheted, missing Salt's head by an inch. Loretta let out a *squack* and flew straight out of the hole. The second rock knocked the bone saw clean out of Aunt Mary Athena's grip.

"Jeez, Dr. Salt," said Candi, a voice out of the shadowy darkness at the opposite end of the sinkhole. "You got a great grip for . . . what? Human? Dragon? That was a two-rocker."

Aunt Mary Athena hissed angrily. She hissed and hissed. The sound spiraled out of the sinkhole into the bright blue sky above. It met a second, more thoughtful hiss echoing down from above.

Salt looked up. Loretta strutted back and forth across the grassy edge. Next to her, Queenie peered into the sinkhole. Her tongue flickered briefly, smelling the air, smelling Salt's distress. Silently, the dragon withdrew.

Aunt Mary Athena wheeled around. "I yam sicka yew," she hissed toward Candi's part of the darkness. "Yew and yewr pupurle mineeskurt and yewr blew eye shadow and yewr idiot dream to go to Parisss."

"Oh yeah? Oh YEAH?" yelled Candi. She poked her head over a boulder and glared at Aunt Mary Athena.

The moment Aunt Mary Athena turned to face Candi, Sparky appeared at the lip of the sinkhole. Down he flowed, tail curling around an outcropping here and there, his iridescent wings partially opened for balance.

Candi grabbed a fresh chunk of coal and went into her windup. She threw high and inside, aiming to dust Aunt Mary Athena back.

"OW!" bellowed his aunt.

"Well, you, Dr. Salt, are just another grasping, self-absorbed person from East Nowhere, Ohio, same as me! Just because you're gonna spend the rest of your life eating raw cow instead of those stupid vegetable pills and laying eggs in a smelly old cave somewhere doesn't mean you can make fun of my life's goals!"

"Oooooo!" bellowed Dr. Salt. "Yew . . . yew . . . Candi!"

"Hey," said Candi. "You remembered my name. 'Bout time."

As he neared the bottom, Sparky opened his wings a little and glided the last ten feet. Silently, he landed next to Salt. Salt reached out and scratched the dragon behind the ear folds. Sparky undulated pleasurably from head to tail. And at that moment, as clearly as if Sparky had spoken actual words, Salt knew what he was supposed to do. The dragons had a plan.

"Had I opposable thums, I wood pick up the saw bone and saw yew," roared Aunt Mary Athena.

Salt put his hand under his sprained kneecap and carefully eased onto Sparky's back.

Candi crossed her arms. "You know, Dr. Salt, it kills me that of all the cute little animals you could have turned yourself into, you picked the scaliest, snoutiest, snaggle-toothiest around. Kinda antibeauty culture, doncha think?"

With a roar, Aunt Mary Athena lunged for Candi. Candi pitched another chunk.

"OW!"

Sparky's powerful muscles contracted. His wings unfolded with a majestic rustle. Salt laid his cheek against Sparky's ridged backbone.

"You'll live with the pack!" screeched Candi. "Practice mutual grooming! You couldn't stand the thought of just one measly assistant—now you'll be a part of a rigid social hierarchy that instinctually bands together to ensure the survival of the species! You're gonna hate it!"

Sparky snaked up the steep rock face. As he neared the top, his wings began to beat in time to his caterpillar crawl. Salt's heart leaped. What if? What if Sparky? Would Sparky actually? Maybe, you know . . . fly?

The last twenty feet were taken in a glorious rush of wings and speed. Sparky burst out of the sinkhole in full flight while Salt clung to his back. Joyous, humble pride filled Salt's soul. The dragons had chosen him—John Salt, moderately brave guy—to experience Ohio's first manned dragonflight.

"Yeeee-HHHAAAAHHH!" yelled Salt.

The morning sun was dead ahead. Salt blinked, blinked, blinked, trying to contract his pupils. Sparky climbed through the bright blue sky, his wings churning the air into a sweet song rushing past Salt's ears. A wing stroke brushed Salt's swollen kneecap. It felt like a blessing, a benediction.

"Lookit MEEEEE!"

Down below, the Wilds spread out like a miniature world. Sparky dive-bombed the giraffes . . .

"I'M FLY—"

caused a stampede among the scimitar-horned oryxes . . .

"Whoa, whoa, WHOA!"

and turned loop-the-loops over the Jackson's antelopes.

Salt closed his eyes and hung on for dear life. "Okay. I'm done now," he whimpered. "You can let me off."

As they came out of the barrel roll over the panicking elands, Pal, Rascal, Smokey, and Trigger soared into formation behind them. Where were the other dragons, the females? Salt looked down. There they were on the ground far, far below, slithering into the sinkhole, Queenie in the lead.

Uh-oh. Salt had forgotten about Mary Athena. His heart lurched. His—um, aunt? Dragon? What?—was still in that sinkhole. And Candi? Salt's knee throbbed. While it was all fun and flying up here, Candi was still deep underground, surrounded by dragons.

Salt leaned to the right and pointed downward. "This way, men!" he shouted. "We've got to go back and rescue Candi! She'll be scared stiff, and—wait a minute! I said—hey! Turn around! Where do you think you're going? Bad Sparky! Down! Back! I said, GO BACK!"

But the flying wedge of dragons, Salt furiously yelling commands, sailed merrily away from the sinkhole and headed toward the town of Spratt.

Chapter Eighteen

—⁓—

Meanwhile, back at the sinkhole, Candi could not believe her eyes. John Salt, the big weenie, was taking off! Leaving her to fight Dr. Salt all by herself!

She cupped her hands around her mouth and yelled, "You come back here this second, Salt! SA-LT! I could use a little of your stupid help, ya know!"

Not that he paid any attention to her. He and that dumb dragon just kept going, flying straight out of the sinkhole and leaving her holding the bag. Boy, wasn't *that* just typical? Show a guy a little in-depth scientific reasoning, a little superior rock throwing, and the guy bailed. Every time.

"Well, that is just too darned bad, Salt," yelled Candi. "Because I am done playing cute and perky and slightly dumb all the time. Like it or lump it."

Dr. Salt (The dragon? What?) undulated ever closer.

Candi whomped her again with a rock from her ammo pile and ducked behind the boulder. Shoot. Her brand-new jeans had a big hole in the knee. If she got out of this alive, her mom was going to kill her.

"Like it or lump it, yissss," agreed Dr. Salt. "Hee will not be back. That matters not. I yam dragon meat now. My dwindling side of human wants to kill yew. But now as dragon, I wish to stalk a cow, merely." Dr. Salt's tongue flicked, tasting the air. "No time left in reversing the process. My arms aire gone, my legs aire fused—do I not have a loverly tail spike?"

Candi peeked over her boulder. "Sure. It's nice," she said.

"I loose the capacity to speak. Soon, think in human will I not. I bask in the sun and dream in dragon, only. But I tell yew a last one thing."

Candi stood up cautiously, a rock in each hand. Just in case. "What?"

"Parisss," whispered Dr. Salt. "Tonight."

"Huh?"

"Yissss. Thaire isss my plane ticket. Keys to my apartment. Money, yiss, yiss. Sitting on the table of my lab. Yew can have it all. I gifffft to yew."

A rock slipped from Candi's hand. "Paris?" she breathed. "I can go to Paris—on your plane? Tonight?"

"Yisss."

Candi's eyes grew round. "And stay at your apart-ment?"

"Yisss."

"And go to the cosmetics show?" squealed Candi. The rock slipped out of her other hand.

"Ssssstay," agreed Dr. Salt. "As long as yew like. I insissst."

Candi grinned happily. "Boy, oh boy, oh *boy*! Thanks, Dr. Salt!"

Dr. Salt was turning out not to be such a bad person—um, dragon—after all. Except for the part about murdering that poor dragon and trying to do the same to her nephew, but hey, everybody makes mis-takes, right? And Paris—boy, oh boy, oh boy!

Dr. Salt snaked close. And closer. "One thing last. A thing yew will do for me, poooor me that is turning into a dragon, nevair again will I see Parisss." Her self-pitying snout loomed over the boulder. "One thing. Take the black leather backpack—*très* chik, no?—that lay on the dissecting table in my lab." Dr. Salt's scales rippled in a shrug. "Isss ticket, keys, money. Also a package. Deliver this package to my office. They will know what to do." Dr. Salt dropped her snout and hissed softly. "Nothing this isss. This is nothing. A research scientist's wish at the lassst."

Three dragons slithered down from corners of the

sinkhole. They rolled Dr. Salt over and over, nosing her, tasting her. Welcoming her to the pack. There was a small *pop* as the string broke and Dr. Salt's pearls pattered to the ground. The metamorphosis was complete.

Candi climbed onto the boulder and gazed happily at the roiling sea of dragons just below her platform sneakers. Gosh, who would have thought? This whole thing was turning out great. The dragons were okay. Salt was rescued. And she was on her way to Paris. France. Whoa.

Wrapped in her happy dream, Candi scrambled over the lip of the sinkhole and looked down. It was way easy to figure out which dragon used to be Dr. Mary Athena Salt. She? (It? What?) reared up authoritatively over the other dragons, a permanently annoyed look on its face.

Biking back to Spratt was absolutely fabulous. Fluffy little clouds chased one another across the totally turquoise sky. The breeze blew cheerfully through the scraggy grass and pricker bushes. Candi hummed a little French tune. *"Dormay-vooo, Dormay-vooo."*

Boy, oh boy, oh boy. Pale and perfect and draped across the Pont Neuf. Dressed in black and glamorous, touring Versailles, walking in the footsteps of Madame du Barry and all the little du Barrys. Pale, pouting, black, perfect at the cosmetics show. Perfect.

Her humming trailed off. Candi frowned. Black, white, pale, pouting, black, frozen. Funny. This day-dream was like . . . color-blind.

Candi daydreamed harder. Instead of morphing into full color, though, her dream continued with an annoyed-looking dragon that slithered arrogantly over stone bridges and sneered at the ornately framed art-works hanging on the museum walls.

Candi winced as she coasted downhill toward Spratt. Was that the best she could hope for—to see Paris through Dr. Salt's eyes? Because honestly, if being a big deal in makeup meant that she'd have to spend the rest of her life wearing nothing but black while lying, mur-dering, and mixing up people's names—forget it.

Candi rode past St. Mark's. "But I still wanna go to Paris," she murmured as she coasted toward the small crowd gathered around an ambulance in front of the church. The ambulance's swing doors were wide open. Two EMTs were lifting Salt onto a stretcher.

"You okay, Candi?" called Salt weakly.

"Yeah. I'm mad at you for dumping me like that, though," she yelled back.

"I tried to go back. . . . " Salt grimaced as the EMTs strapped him to the gurney. "But Sparky . . ."

"Later, Salt," Candi yelled impatiently as she picked up speed. "I got a lot on my mind right now!"

A bellowing hoot from the top of the church made her look up. Gosh, poor Father Aloysius. He was leaning dangerously far out of the church's belfry, flapping a vestry robe and yelling, "Shoo! Git!" at a dragon curled around the steeple. The dragon rattled its wings and burped out blue flames. A couple of roof slates came loose and crashed to the pavement. The crowd jumped back.

Candi rode past the crowd and on to the Salts' house. She biked up the driveway and stopped just outside Dr. Salt's garage lab.

The garage doors were open, the lights burning. And there, like a deep, dark hole in the middle of the stainless steel table, was a black leather backpack propped against an empty kitchen bowl.

Thoughtfully, Candi unpacked the backpack. In addition to a first-class plane ticket, a set of house keys, and five thousand euros, she found a small, brown package addressed to the Research and Development Lab, Orléans World Headquarters, Paris, France.

"Hmm. I bet I know what's inside this package," Candi remarked to the beautiful leather backpack. "What's inside this package is the last of poor Blackie or whoever, and a bunch of advice about figuring out the appropriate ratio of human-to-dragon blood serum.

"And dragons will be the next animal hunted to the

brink of extinction for the sake of human vanity." Candi sighed heavily. "Like rhinos for their horns, and elephants for their tusks. Salt is right. Animal experimentation stinks. That time in evolutionary biology? I should have let *my* fruit flies go too.

"So I'm certainly not going to participate in any more of Dr. Salt's evil schemes. But I can still go to Paris, see? All I gotta do is go and say to the people in the research lab, 'Package? What package?' And then—" Candi's breath caught as she pulled out from the bottom of the pack Dr. Salt's killer gorgeous iTellit grommet belt.

"Dr. Salt thought I was just a kid," mumured Candi. "A cute and perky and slightly dumb kid. And that I'd follow her anywhere because I wanted to be like her." She stroked the oversized metal buckle and sighed. "And I did, at first. But now—now I know that the reason I got into makeup in the first place is because of the gorgeous colors. All those pots and tubes and brushes to express without words what I see, how I feel, what I mean when I look at the world. . . ." Candi blinked, astonished.

"Like an artist," she whispered, suddenly aware. "Like a painter. But exactly."

She picked up the plane ticket, stared at it a moment, then slowly tore it in two. "Why should I go to Paris as a makeup lady," she whispered, "when in a couple of years I could go as a painter. An artist. Whoa, infinitely cooler."

Candi clasped the grommet belt to her chest in triumph. "And I'll get there, someday, somehow!" she cried. "'Cause every artist goes to Paris at least once in her lifetime!"

Chapter Nineteen

One week later, on the morning of the thirty-first, John Salt slumped down on the Clarkes' living room couch and eavesdropped on the conversation going on in the dining room.

"Stop wiggling around, Allison," said Candi.

"Sorry. I thought I heard the door slam. Your brother should be home from his baseball game soon, huh?"

"Shoot. I'm having trouble controlling your skin tones. And there's something not quite right about your eyes." Salt heard the sound of a book opening and the flip-flip of pages turning. He knew exactly what book Candi Clarke was looking at. *Beginning Oil Painting Techniques*. She flipped through it a hundred times a day.

"Candi, this is deeply boring. We could be doing stuff," said Allison.

Allison's voice. Such an arrow in his heart. Salt

slumped lower. His left elbow jostled the crutches leaning against the arm of the couch.

He had stayed at the Clarkes' house for a week, long enough for the whole, ugly truth to dawn. In a lot of ways, his life was bleaker now than when he had been stuck at the bottom of the forty-foot sinkhole. At least a week ago, he had still had his hopes, still had his dreams. And now?

His knee ached. Salt shifted, trying to find a more comfortable slump. His elbow knocked a crutch to the floor.

"Salt! Keep it quiet in there! I'm trying to concentrate!" yelled Candi.

"Yeah, yeah," muttered Salt.

Easy for her to concentrate. She was totally wrapped up in her painting. Nothing else mattered.

His situation was totally different. A lot of things mattered. Salt had all sorts of problems—big problems, little problems. Early that morning, for instance, Mr. Clarke had driven to Columbus to meet his parents' plane. Salt was not looking forward to seeing them again, even though he sort of missed them a lot. First, his parents were sure to make a big, embarrassing deal out of his sprained kneecap when the doctor already said it would heal up fine. Next, they'd get all hurt and wounded because Aunt Mary Athena, that great old gal, had flown back to Paris without a word to anybody. At least, that's what everybody thought. At least, that's what Candi had told them. Sort of.

"Um. I don't think you'll be able to reach her," she had told her parents that Sunday evening after they had brought Salt home from the emergency room and settled him down on the couch. "Dr. Salt told me her plane left tonight. For Paris. France. You know." She gave her parents a big, cheesy smile. Ham had snorted, but Mr. and Mrs. Clarke bought it.

"Well, I'm sure she had her reasons," said Mrs. Clarke. "Some work crisis or another." She fluffed up a couch pillow and tucked the afghan around Salt's knees. "You can stay right here with us, John, until your folks get back."

That part had worked out great, actually. With his aunt out of the picture, Salt had spent the week on the Clarkes' couch, within easy hobbling distance of the kitchen. A whole week of Mrs. Clarke's truly outstanding cooking. Definitely not a problem.

On the other hand, by the time Candi remembered to tell him about her phone conversation with his dad, it was too late to do anything about the grass. So his parents' VIP houseguest was going to wade through knee-deep grass just to get to the front door. His dad was *not* going to be happy about that.

Then there was Allison Fishbinder.

Salt had spent every day after school on the Clarkes' couch, watching Baseball Hall of Fame videos with Ham and pretending to do his homework. Allison came over every afternoon. At first Salt figured she came over to hang out with Candi. But Candi was completely wrapped up in her oil paints and one of Mr. Eggebean's extra-credit science projects. She barely came out of her room for meals.

Which didn't seem to bother Allison. She kept coming over anyway. She just planted herself in the living room chair and watched baseball videos with the guys.

And hope had squeezed Salt's heart. Maybe . . . maybe he, John Salt, was the reason Allison kept glancing over to the couch?

By Wednesday afternoon, though, it was painfully clear: Girls picked the sports hero over the moderately brave guy every time—and Ham was the best baseball player Spratt had. By Friday Salt began to wonder if maybe Ham wasn't glancing back. It wouldn't surprise him. Life was so unfair.

Salt picked up the crutches, hoisted himself onto his feet, and swung into the dining room. Candi had set up her portable easel on the long wooden table. Allison Fishbinder sat on a kitchen stool placed directly in front of the big bay window. She looked exactly like an angel, if angels yawned and picked indifferently at their nail polish.

Salt swallowed painfully. If Ham held the key to Allison's heart—well, Salt wouldn't stand in the way. Love was complicated enough without ruining your best friendship over it.

Candi glanced at him, then back at her canvas. Dressed in lemon yellow tie-dye and green overalls, with her frizzy hair piled high on her head and her face scrubbed free of makeup, Candi looked . . . moderately cute.

Salt blinked, astonished.

"I'm missing some crucial element in Allison's eyes," she said to him, tapping her teeth with the handle of her paintbrush. "My book says a painted portrait is supposed to be a portrait of the subject's innermost being, but if that's true, Allison is in big trouble."

Allison gave an offended sniff. "Candi, c'mon. Let's *do* something."

"One more minute," Candi murmured, frowning at her painting.

"I mean, all you ever want to do anymore is this weenie painting stuff," continued Allison, her eyes narrowing. "And all that stuff you're doing for Mr. Eggebean, like you're . . . smart or something."

"Like it or lump it, Allison," said Candi. "I am what I

am. Hmm. Maybe if I shade with a little burnt sienna and cover up that weird mole on her neck . . ."

"Hey!" cried Allison. "I heard that! I have excellent hearing, and I heard that! I do *not* have a weird mole on my neck! It's a beauty mark! There's a big difference!" She crossed her arms. "Boy. Kathi O'Dell sure doesn't talk about me like that," she muttered. "Kathi is totally cool about everything."

The dining room door banged open. Ham, still in his dirty ball uniform and spikes, clacked through the door.

"Five to four, Salt," Ham grumbled, taking his cap off and throwing it on the table. "We woulda won if that stupid ump woulda called half the freakin'—"

Allison jumped up. "Hiya, Ham." She fluffed up her hair and beamed at him.

Ham blushed. "Hey, Allison."

Salt's heart sank. So it was true. Allison liked Ham. Ham liked Allison. Of all the lousy happy endings.

The dining room door banged open again—and there stood his parents.

"Sweetie!" cried Salt's mom.

Okay, so it was pretty cool to see his folks again. His mom raced over to hug him hard, laughing and crying and visibly restraining herself from kissing him in public, thank goodness. One of his crutches clattered to the floor.

"Good grief, John. You had us worried," said his dad, coming up on the other side and strangling Salt's elbow in a death grip. His dad's eyes were sort of shiny, and he was clearing his throat a lot. Salt got the message.

"Ever since the Clarkes called and told us what happened," agreed his mom, "I've barely slept a wink. Thank goodness you're okay, more or less. Shouldn't you be sitting down, though?"

"I'm fine, Mom," said Salt. "It's no big deal, honest."

The Clarkes squeezed into the dining room, followed by his parents' VIP from Washington. The VIP, a small, dark man dressed in black leather jeans and a motorcycle jacket, picked up Salt's crutch and handed it back to him. Salt turned to put out his hand—and found himself eyeball to eyeball with the great man himself.

"Dr. Zhao?" he whispered.

"Oh, sweetie, let me introduce you," exclaimed Salt's mom. "Dr. Zhao arrived at the Chinese embassy two days after we got to Washington. We didn't say anything because we wanted to surprise you."

Dr. Zhao shook Salt's outstretched hand. "Happy to meet a fellow field researcher."

Salt shook back, his slightly broken heart totally forgotten in the thrill of meeting the world's foremost dragonologist face to face. "Wow, Dr. Zhao! What an honor to meet you, sir! Just—*wow*!" Dr. Zhao grinned.

"And you will never believe what happened on the flight into Columbus," said Salt's mom. "The guy in the seat next to Dr. Zhao was none other than Truman Hackett—he's the chairman of the State Finance Committee. Dr. Zhao pulled out his wallet and showed him your dragon pictures, John. Hackett loved 'em."

Dr. Zhao nodded at Ham. "I gave him the one of you, scratching Pal's back with a stick."

Allison beamed at Ham. Ham beamed at Allison. Salt tried to remain philosophical.

"Anyway, by the time we landed, Hackett promised to push through dragon funding for the next fiscal year." Salt's mom rubbed her hands together and gloated. "The Wilds is rich!"

"Why, SueAnn, that's terrific," exclaimed Mrs. Clarke. "Why don't we all go into the kitchen and celebrate? I got some in-a-minute cookies ready for the oven, and there's a pot of fresh coffee." Still chattering, Mrs. Clarke led the way into the kitchen.

Salt's nose twitched. Ordinarily, he would have fought to be first in line for cookies, but he wanted to spend every minute with his personal hero, and Dr. Zhao had wandered over to the dining room windows. He and Candi were huddled over Allison's portrait, deep in talk. Salt stumped over.

"Hmm," Dr. Zhao was saying. "Great use of color. But

your line tones need work, and you are never going to get anywhere with such sloppy drawing."

He straightened. "Get John, here, to give you some drawing lessons. The boy's a natural draftsman."

"Salt?" said Candi. "Really?"

"I pinned your portrait of Rusty to the wall next to my desk at the research station," said Dr. Zhao. "It's beautiful. Anatomically accurate *and* a work of art. I must look at it a hundred times a day."

Candi eyed Salt, surprised. "That's right, you like to draw. I guess I never paid much attention."

Salt shrugged modestly, but the way Candi was looking at him made his heart beat a little faster.

Dr. Zhao frowned at Candi's painting. "Your biggest problem is that you're working the paint as if that's all it was—shiny stuff you squeeze out of a tube and smear any old way over a piece of canvas."

He took the paintbrush out of Candi's hand. He leaned over the table and examined the row of paint tubes tucked neatly through the many loops of a long, smooth stretch of white leather with an oversized metal buckle at one end—Salt grinned. His aunt's fashionable utility belt was Candi's new paint caddy. Dr. Zhao selected a couple of tubes and filled the brush with white and soft yellow.

"Now watch," he whispered reverently, and leaned

into Candi's painting. "It's not paint anymore, is it?" He brushed a tiny fleck of color into the corner of Allison's eyes. Suddenly there was Allison, right inside the paint, rolling her eyes and complaining about square dancing.

Candi's jaw dropped. "Of course . . . of course—the light shining in her eyes! An artist isn't working with *paint*, she's working with *light*!"

Candi grabbed the painting from the easel and twirled around the dining room table, holding it up to see. "Hey, I get it, I really get it!"

"Bravo, Miss ah—"

"It's Candi," said Candi. "With an 'i'."

"Candi. Got it. You know, Candi, most painters never see beyond the paint to the light," he said. "I should know. I studied art as well as zoology during my student days in Oxford."

"You did?" said Salt.

"You did?" echoed Candi. She eyed Dr. Zhao's motor-cycle jacket. "Hmm. So a person can be talented in both science and art and still dress pretty cool, huh?"

Dr. Zhao smiled modestly. "Don't get the wrong idea. I'm just a Sunday painter. Dragon research keeps me pretty busy. But I could probably give you both a few pointers while I'm here."

"Wow," whispered Salt. "Just—*wow*."

"Boy, oh boy, oh boy!" exclaimed Candi. "Thanks, Dr.

Zhao!" She tilted the painting up to the windows to admire the wet spots on Allison's eyes.

The delicious smell of brown sugar and toasting peanuts filled the air. Dr. Zhao inhaled deeply. "A mother who bakes," he said. "My favorite." He winked at Salt, then made off for the cookies in the kitchen.

Candi punched Salt on the shoulder. "Gosh, Salt, I'm so happy I'm gonna bust! A real artist—right here in Spratt!"

Her eyes narrowed. "I wonder if Dr. Zhao needs an assistant while he's here. Okay, sure, assisting didn't work out so great last time, but I've dropped the cute and slightly dumb act, and I *know* an artist needs somebody to bring them coffee and sort brushes and stuff." Candi eyed Salt. "Hmm. Maybe I should be assisting *you*, Salt."

Salt shrugged.

Candi regarded him. "You're really not going to tell anybody the truth about your aunt, are you?"

Salt shifted on his crutches. "Well, everybody thinks my aunt is back in France. And nobody noticed Blackie's disappearance. The animal techs just came to work on Monday and started calling Aunt Mary Athena 'Blackie.' Heck, *I've* started calling Aunt Mary Athena 'Blackie.' She seems to like it. It's weird, though. Aunt Mary Athena has a very unremarkable ridge pattern formation while the real Blackie had three distinct trapezoidal markings transverse across the fourth vertebra, so you'd think—"

"Sa-alt," said Candi warningly.

"Well. They don't look anything alike. But it's true that Aunt Mary Athena has taken Blackie's place in the dragon pack. And she's happy. After all, dragons live for a thousand years. So in dragon years Aunt Mary Athena is just a kid, and isn't that what she wanted? To be young again?"

Candi snorted. "Plus, she makes a better dragon than she ever did a human being."

She put the oil painting back on the easel and stepped back, smiling at it. "Hey, you know that big old buckeye tree by the ball diamond? I snuck out last night and buried the package with what was left of Blackie underneath it. Dug way down into the slimy worm part, as far down as I could get."

"Safe underground at last. Blackie would have appreciated it. Thanks, Candi."

She nodded, her smile going soft and dreamy. "Mmm. Ya know, Salt, it's like all my life I've been half asleep. Working so hard at being popular; spending so much time with makeup. All that perkiness and cuteness and dumbness—I was just going through the motions. But now, see, with painting, it's like—it's like—"

"Like the piece of you that was missing all your life

suddenly showed up," said Salt matter-of-factly, tapping his rib bones. "Right here." Candi's jaw dropped. "What? What are you staring at? Do I have dirt on my face?"

"Jeez, Salt, that's it exactly! Like finding the missing piece!" She looked him up and down like she'd never seen him before. "Funny, how you and me ended up at the same place, isn't it? From, like, opposite ends of Planet Popular, here we are, all wrapped up in art and science and Dr. Zhao. . . ."

Her voice trailed off as she eyed his *I Brake for Animals* T-shirt and double chin and the naturally goofy expression on his face. "Well. Maybe not *exactly* the same place. Okay, sure, so I'm not the second-most-popular girl in Spratt anymore—I'm probably down to fourth or fifth, huh?—but you're okay. To me, at least. Plus, coming up with a great plan at the bottom of a sinkhole like that, whoa. Pretty smart."

Candi cocked her head, considering him. "Brave, too. Brave to protect the dragons like that. You have the courage of your convictions, Salt. Like that time in evolutionary biology? I should have backed you up on that fruit fly thing."

Salt could hardly believe his ears. "You think I'm brave? Really?"

"Yeah, I do," said Candi firmly. "'*Cogito, ergo sum.*' C'mon. Let's get into the kitchen and grab some cookies before Ham and Allison leave us nothing but a plate full of crumbs."

Salt watched her breeze out of the room. Candi thought he was brave. Candi thought he was smart. Candi was all wrapped up in art and science and Dr. Zhao too. Boy.

Could it be possible that a girl like Candi and a guy like Salt—?

Well . . . why not? Everything they had done, everything they had gone through together, had been a deeply personal bonding experience. And they were definitely going to be spending a lot of time together, hanging out with Dr. Zhao and learning about art. So it was possible, maybe, by the time the seventh grade dance rolled around next month . . . with a little dragon's luck . . .

Coolly, casually, Salt stumped after her.

Author's Note

—⁓—

Although I made up this story, the setting is based on a real place. There really is a wildlife park called the International Center for the Preservation for Wildlife—the Wilds—located in southern Muskingum County, Ohio. It's about forty-five minutes from my front door here in Zanesville, if I roll down all the car windows and drive really fast east on Route 146.

Some of the tallest reticulated giraffes (they're kind of stuck-up about it), the laziest Bactrian camels (I swear, the only thing I've ever seen the camels do is sleep), and the sassiest southern white rhinos (sometimes they charge the safari busses! Yikes!) on the planet are found on the fourteen square miles of reclaimed coal land that make up the Wilds.

I hope someday you can visit the Wilds either in person or online at www.thewilds.org. It's one of my favorite places—and I hope it'll be one of yours, too.

—Linda Zinnen
Zanesville, Ohio